H.N. WAKE
ECHOES OF THUNDER

BOOKS

Vinci Books

vinci-books.com

Published by Vinci Books Ltd in 2025

1

Copyright © H.N. Wake 2023

The author has asserted their moral right to be identified as the author of this work in accordance with the Copyright, Designs and Patents Act 1988. This work is a work of fiction. Names, characters, places and incidents are the product of the author's imagination or are used fictitiously. Any resemblance to actual persons, living or dead, places and incidents is entirely coincidental.

All rights reserved. No part of this publication may be copied, reproduced, distributed, stored in any retrieval system, or transmitted in any form or by any means, including photocopying, recording, or other electronic or mechanical methods, nor used as a source for any form of machine learning including AI datasets, without the prior written permission of the publisher.

The publisher and the author have made every effort to obtain permissions for any third party material used in this book and to comply with copyright law. Any queries in this respect should be brought to the attention of the publisher and any omissions will be corrected in future editions.

A CIP catalogue record for this book is available from the British Library.

Paperback ISBN: 9781036704865

The EU GPSR authorised representative is Logos Europe, 9 rue Nicolas Poussion, 17000 La Rochelle, France contact@logoseurope.eu

By H.N. Wake

FBI Agent Domini Walker

Sound of a Furious Sky
Hidden in the Silence
Secrets of the Angels
Echoes of Thunder

For those who refuse to quit.

They shut me up in Prose—
As when a little Girl
They put me in the Closet—
Because they liked me "still"—

Still! Could themself have peeped—
And seen my Brain—go round—
They might as wise have lodged a Bird
For Treason—in the Pound—

Himself has but to will
And easy as a Star
Look down upon Captivity—
And laugh—No more have I—

Emily Dickinson

Prologue

Seven years ago

Mila Pascale's mother had been drunk for seventy-one hours. That was 4,260 minutes that her mother had been lying in the bed with the coffee mug of vodka. It had also been seventy-one hours since the police had first arrived.

Mila stood in the bedroom doorway. "It's about to officially be hour seventy-two."

Her mother squinted to focus. "What?"

"That will be 259,200 seconds." Mila liked the stability of numbers.

Her mother's forehead wrinkled.

"The FBI says the first seventy-two hours are the most critical." Mila's anger spiked and her heart thumped rashly. Exasperated, she rushed the words. "Seventy-two, Mother. Seventy-two. The FBI says that's the time to secure evidence, talk to witnesses. They say kidnappers hurt kids early. Seventy-four percent of stolen children are dead within three hours." She took a breath. Being the smartest in the family led to many frustrations. Many. She slowed her words. "That means their chances of them finding Jimmy are diminishing."

Her mother looked away. She didn't want to hear the numbers. She didn't want to hear a lot of things. Not now.

Mila stepped backward into the hallway.

She'd been the one to print out ten variations of Jimmy's photo. It was Mila who'd delivered them personally to the elementary school principal. It had also been Mila who'd shared a photo on numerous Facebook groups, including one for hobbyists who chased missing persons. Yesterday, she'd printed full-sized photos and stapled them on light posts across the neighborhood. Fourteen-year-olds could do a lot.

She turned toward Jimmy's room. The door was closed. Jimmy never closed his door. Ten-year-old boys didn't close doors. They wanted to be with the pack.

Walking slowly down the hall, she counted one foot in front of the other as she had since she and her brother had been little. Nine steps. Always nine. The permanent dimensions of the floor in relation to the variability of her growing legs meant that even if she shortened or lengthened her stride, it was still nine steps to Jimmy's room.

She stood in front of Jimmy's door and placed her palm against the wood. The characteristics of wood made it the same as the ambient temperature. Always room temperature. Unlike skin. Skin temperature changed depending on both internal and external factors. What temperature was Jimmy's skin right now? Was he running at top speed to escape someone, his skin bright red and burning? Was he bound tightly in thick wool? Or was he being held under frigid water?

She may never again know what Jimmy was feeling. Because according to FBI statistics, he wasn't ever coming home.

Part I

Chapter One

Students filed into the large lecture hall of New York University's Waverly Building, dropped into seats, and pulled out laptops. On the stage, Professor Irawaddy stepped to the podium and set down his notes. He was a graceful, slight man with small shoulders and deeply black hair over a thin face. Even from the audience, his nose appeared long below wire-rimmed glasses. The fact that he never smiled added gravitas to his already very serious subjects. But his tone was always gentle and patient, as if he had raised many girls. Behind him, the large screen clicked to life.

Irawaddy was Mila Pascale's favorite professor. She appreciated individuals who were passionate about their specialty. This particular Criminal Justice Administration course had so far proven to be the foundational learning she had wanted for her career in the FBI. Over the last two months, Irawaddy had intertwined the dry issues of law enforcement management, policies, and procedures with exciting examples from the field. Last week, the title of his lecture had been "Technology in Use" and he had covered the work of the FBI's Operational Technology Division section that provided tech capabilities across the breadth of the Bureau's departments, from intelligence to national security. She had taken prodigious notes on their audio, video, and imaging support, including advanced electronic surveillance of wireless and data network communications. They also processed and collected counter-encryption and digital evidence. She imagined men in white lab coats breaking into computers.

Irawaddy clicked on the microphone and the students quieted.

The lecture title flashed on the screen. "Inter Agency Cooperation on Human Trafficking."

Like a fog bank, cold moved up through her chest.

His voice was raspy. "Since 2007, the National Human Trafficking Hotline has received over twenty-two thousand reports of sex trafficking cases. Of these, likely one in six missing and exploited children are endangered runaways. Globally, there are approximately 4.5 million people trapped in forced sexual exploitation. Roughly two million are children. It is a lucrative industry making an estimated ninety-nine billion dollars a year."

As if on its own accord, Mila's right hand reached down into her courier bag and clamped around a pen. There was no need for her to take notes on the laptop. She knew the stats.

The next slide was a graph detailing the demographic categories of missing children.

The fog slithered through her arms to her fingers. Holding the pen scissored between her index and middle finger, she twitched it back and forth in an even, staccato rhythm. Back, forth, back, forth.

As if from another room, Irawaddy's distant voice said, "In forty percent of stereotypical kidnappings, the child will be killed."

Back, forth, back, forth. She glanced to the left wall and focused on the brightness emanating from a wall sconce.

"We've seen that almost eighty-five percent of the perpetrators are male."

It had been 2,601 days since Jimmy had disappeared.

"Abducted children are predominantly female."

It wasn't healthy for her to count the days. But once she had started, it had been impossible to stop. It was just the way her brain worked. It hooked on to numbers, patterns, and rhythms. She had an obsessive personality and could get stuck on an idea or a goal. Before they had diagnosed her as being on the spectrum, a teacher had once described her as *stubborn like a pit bull*. Stubborn. Actually, she didn't mind the comparison to a pit bull because they were fearless and intentional. But her stubbornness wasn't a chosen character trait. Like being bossy. It was hardwired. Immutable. Her unique traits would also be an asset. Especially for the Bureau.

Irawaddy's voice was muffled. "Nearly half of all victims are sexually assaulted."

The thumping of her heart felt like a hammer trying to break her ribcage from the inside. The anxiety was swelling.

She set the pen down with a bang louder than she had intended. The neighboring student glanced over. Mila closed her eyes. *Breathe, breathe. Ten, nine, eight.*

An imaginary ghost brushed her wrist. Her mind stilled and her heart calmed as she welcomed the daydream and the illusory feel of Jimmy's hand on her arm. In the recurring memory, she was fourteen and walking Jimmy the four blocks to his school. He was talking about the show-and-tell session his class would have the next week.

His bright-blue eyes had been full of seriousness. "Lala, you need to help me." As a baby, he had mispronounced her name as "Lala" and it had stuck. "I really don't know what to bring."

She tried to smooth his cowlick the way Mother always did. "It's about showing the other kids something you really like."

Giving her a deep shrug, the bright yellow of his soccer shirt on his shoulders reached his ears. He pleaded, "Like what?"

"What do you like?"

His shoulders dropped emphatically. "Spaghetti and meatballs."

The logic was sound. He loved the past-due, discounted spaghetti and meatballs they purchased as takeout at the local deli. It felt as if they'd discovered a sneaky way to eat at a fancy restaurant. "That's not a bad idea."

He grinned widely.

"But, I mean, kinda all kids like spaghetti and meatballs."

He nodded sadly. "Sure. You're right. All kids love spaghetti and meatballs."

"What if you talk about something that's really valuable to you, something that others don't know much about?"

Up ahead at the corner, the crossing guard in a neon green vest was corralling a group of kids.

Jimmy said, "I mean, some of my Hot Wheels are really the best."

She gave him a questioning look.

He frowned. "All kids like Hot Wheels?"

"Don't they?"

"Yeah. I guess they do."

"I think you need something that is special to you."

He turned to her. "Lala, can I bring *you* into class?"

Jimmy was the nicest, kindest kid. She hugged his small shoulders and laughed. "Nope. Keep thinking."

She released his hand as they approached the waiting crowd.

He raised a finger. "I got it! The Rice Krispie treats that mix the sprinkles with the chocolate and white chocolate chips!"

It had been his own concoction. She nodded heavily. "That's a great idea. Very special. Very *Jimmy*. We can make it the night before. Ask Ms. Griffen today if you can bring that in and share with the class."

He punched the air with a fist and his wide smile showed off two big rabbit teeth. "Perfect! Thanks, Lala!"

The light changed and the bustling group of kids surged across the pedestrian walk.

He had given her a wave. "See ya later, alligator!"

From the stage, back in the present day, Irawaddy said, "Well, folks, that's all for today."

She took a deep breath to clear the tightness in her chest and felt the chilled fog dissipate from her veins.

He turned off the overhead screen and pushed down his glasses. "Please remember a few things as you get ready for the first exam in two weeks."

Around Mila, the class groaned. At the top of the laptop screen, a "new mail" icon began to blink. Most students turned off Wi-Fi in lectures to avoid distractions, but Mila knew her strengths and weaknesses: If she'd set a rule, she stuck by it. Her self-imposed structures were a source of pride. She may have been bad with people, but she was really good with rules. She ignored the blinking icon.

Irawaddy continued. "Remember to review the subjects going back to the first day. I will be putting in some questions on the administrative aspects, including budgeting, authorizations, and state and federal oversight."

The class groaned again. The neighboring student whispered, "Crap."

Irawaddy held up a hand. "I know, it's not glamorous, but you need to know who butters the bread of our agencies. That's a very important big-picture item." He rested his palms on the podium. "You can always connect with your teaching assistants if you have any questions. Have a good afternoon."

Around the hall, students snapped laptops closed and rustled through their backpacks.

Mila slid her fingertip across the finger pad and clicked open her inbox.

The sender was info@NCMEC.org and the subject line read, "We have an image for you."

Slamming through her veins like a tsunami, the fog bank returned.

NCMEC stood for the National Center for Missing and Exploited Children, the US clearinghouse for all things related to the prevention of and recovery of children. Every two years, the forensic artists would update a missing child's image to represent their best estimation of the child's current looks. Mila knew that so far, the Forensic Imaging Unit of NCMEC had done around 7,500 age progressions of long-term missing children. This had helped recover 1,800 children.

She blinked against the brightness of the laptop screen.

After the age of eighteen, MCMEC artists only did updates once every five years because at that point, a human face didn't change dramatically. Next year, Jimmy would be eighteen.

She closed the laptop and slid it in her bag.

On the top of a rounded hill in Washington Square Park, a Frisbee game had started. The outside city air smelled of fall's dry leaves. She fished out her phone from a jean pocket and texted Dom, *"Gonna stay in town, sleep @ apartment. Have early class."* It wasn't a lie. She did have an early class the next day.

Six months ago, two corrupt NYPD officers had stalked her Lower East Side apartment. Since escaping, she had been living with Domini and Beecher Walker just outside the city. The lease on the apartment wasn't up for another four months, so she'd been using it as a crash pad for long school days. Dom preferred her to stay in town if her schedule was tough. Dom replied, *"Sure."*

Mila shoved the phone back in the pocket. She did have an early class, but that wasn't why she wanted to stay overnight in the apartment.

She needed to be alone. To quietly view the NCMEC image. Maybe this was the year there would be a crack in the case. Maybe this was the year she found Jimmy.

Chapter Two

Dom Walker sat in the 1966 red Lancia Fulvia Coupé in the short-term parking of Newark Airport's Terminal B. On the ride over, she had noticed a tiny rattle in the engine. She'd need to take a look at that later. The car had been the pride and joy of her late father, NYPD Officer Stewart Walker, and she was religious about its care.

The coffee she'd picked up at a drive-through Dunkin' Donuts was still warm in her hands. She sipped it slowly. She had forty-five minutes yet to kill.

From the seat next to her, her phone rang and she glanced at the screen. It was her Staff Operations Specialist, Lea Peck. She picked up. "Hi."

Lea was young and very smart. She was a huge asset to the Bureau. She was also incredibly sassy and completely unimpressed with most people. She spoke her mind. Her jokes were dirty and her language could be foul. She was also a great friend. "What's the word, morning bird?"

"I just checked the display. The flight is on time. Doesn't arrive for another hour."

Earlier, they had been called into the office of Assistant Director in Charge Yves Fontaine in the FBI Javitz Building near Chinatown. Fontaine, a tall, thin Black man with a Haitian accent and a shrewd mind, had looked up from his desk and set long fingers on wood. "We've got a CI op going down out at Newark." *CI* meant *counterintelligence*. "A South African person of interest is coming in. Agent Walker, I need to insert you for a few hours."

Fontaine wasn't Dom's manager. Her newly assigned supervisor was Barry Lowenstein. But Fontaine and Walker had worked a number of cases over the last few years and he often called her directly. It was common knowledge in Javitz that Walker was one of his favorites. Some grumbled, not so quietly, about it, but Lowenstein knew better than to insert himself into office politics involving Fontaine. Fontaine did office politics better than anyone in the Bureau. Except maybe the Director himself.

Dom had crossed her arms over her chest.

Fontaine had continued. "It's strictly need to know. You're not going to get a lot of details on this one. But it's only a few hours, so there's that."

CI was like that. Compartmentalized, secretive. CI agents stayed to themselves.

He said, "His working name is W. As in W'Kabi."

Lea threw back her head. "Oh, come on."

Dom gave her questioning look.

Lea grumbled, "W'Kabi is a character from the *Black Panther* movie."

Fontaine held up his hands to quiet Lea. "He's in arms trafficking. CI thinks he's a Chinese asset. He slipped his CIA handlers in Joburg. They picked him up again on camera at Istanbul International Airport. He bought a ticket to Newark via Chicago. Arriving on a domestic flight on United."

Dom said, "OK."

"He's arriving in a few hours." He rubbed his chin. "The ops team called. They just got a new, surprising lead. Apparently, his wife and young son are arriving two hours ahead of him with the plan to rendezvous at Newark."

Lea crinkled her face. "Let me guess. Her code name is Nakia."

Fontaine pointed at Lea. "That's enough."

Lea held out her hands as if to say, *And?*

He ignored her and turned back to Dom. "The wife on the move is an unusual pattern. W and his family may be on the run. Permanently. CI don't want to lose him or his connections. She's arriving on American via Hong Kong and Los Angeles. Code name Ladybug."

Lea whispered, "Seriously?"

Dom cleared her throat and Lea clamped her lips shut. Dom cocked her head. "What do you need?"

"If they grab him at Newark and the wife physically protests, they'll take her too."

Lea said it first. "The kid. If they take the target and his wife, they need Dom on the kid."

It was a babysitting job. Dom moved to protest. "Sir—"

Fontaine waved his hands. "I know. We all know. I get it. It's just the CI team doesn't have any women right now."

Lea muttered sarcastically, "You don't say."

Fontaine said, "Peck, pipe it down with the obvious statements. You aren't being clever." He looked back at Dom. "I'm not asking."

An assignment from the boss was an assignment. "Understood. What if they *don't* take the wife?"

"You're free to go."

She asked, "What happens to the kid if they take the wife?"

Fontaine ignored the question and picked up a pen. "Special Agent Peter Cape is in charge. You know him?"

What happens to the kid if they take the wife? Dom said, "Yup."

Fontaine wrote a phone number on a sticky note and handed it to Dom. "Call Cape. And, Lea, I need you doing backup here for Walker."

"Of course, boss." She pointed to her chest. "That's my jam."

He asked Dom, "You OK for a few hours away?"

"Absolutely. We're doing cross-reference on the Salvatore case. All paperwork." The Salvatore case was an indictment of two childcare workers in Brooklyn. Dom and Lea were confirming witness testimony and cleaning documents.

In his office, ASIC Fontaine hadn't mentioned Lowenstein. "Good. Get going."

In the Lancia, Dom took another long sip of coffee.

Lea asked, "Any chatter from the team?"

The CI team was currently located in the Terminal C, where W would be arriving on United from Chicago. "Silence."

"Those guys are scary."

The world of geopolitics, international terrorists, spies, and warfare bred a tight-lipped culture. "They need to be."

Lea whispered, "Gotta be weird to know your target works with the worst individuals in the world." She meant arms trafficking.

"Yup."

"This is not what the Lord wanted his children to be doing. I can tell you that." Lea's father was a Baptist.

"Yup."

"This the first time you've worked with them?"

The CI team housed in Javitz kept to themselves. Followed strict protocols. "Yup."

"Cool. Except for the *lacking of chicks* part. I mean, have you ever met a CI chick?"

"Nope."

"Riffing on the chick, do you think it's the chicken or the egg?"

"What do you mean?"

Lea expanded the thought. "The fact that there are no women in CI. Is that because no sane woman wants to work that shiz or is it because they don't hire any women?"

"I don't know."

"It's so, so old school. Like way back to Victorian times. I'm going to look up their target."

"Lea—"

"Fontaine said I'm backup. So I'm backing up. Don't you want to know something about him?"

"Maybe—" Her phone buzzed against her ear and she glanced at the screen. It was a text from Cape. "I gotta go."

Lea hung up without a word.

Dom opened the message. *"Eyes only. No engagement unless needed. Arr Terminal B from Los Angeles. American Airlines."* He'd attached a photo of a slender Black woman in a black ski coat and jeans holding the hand of a small, Black boy in a red puffer coat. They looked totally normal. A mother and her child. Over her shoulder, the woman had slung a huge, black purse.

What happens to the kid if they take the wife? This wasn't her op. She was here to follow orders. She typed back, *"Copy."*

She set down her coffee, stretched from the car, and picked up an empty backpack from the backseat. No normal civilian went to an airport without a bag.

Inside, standing under the *Arrivals* sign, she texted Cape. *"She's on time. Heading to position."*

She didn't hear back from him.

Chapter Three

Mila let herself into the dark studio apartment on the top floor of a four-story walk-up in Nolita, south of Houston. Through tall windows, streetlights cast bright, white beams across the single armchair, the small table, and the white sheet on the mattress on the floor. A yellow beam from headlights banked off the long wall mirror and lit floating dust motes.

She no longer feared coming here. Dom had assured her that the corrupt, murderous cops had been warned. Dom was a badass. If she'd warned them, they would take heed. Dom and Beecher had given her so much. They had given her a safe and happy home. They had showed her that she could be cared for despite her cumbersome social skills. And although they didn't talk about it much, they had deep reservoirs of understanding about grief, given the death of their father and their abandonment by their mother.

On the counter, she set down the pizza box and large soda from Prince Street. Mila didn't believe in fate. Jimmy's abduction hadn't been his destiny. But finding the Walkers had been some exceptional luck. She tried hard to be a value to them, rather than a burden.

From the lower kitchen cabinet, she retrieved the projector. She opened the windows overlooking Elizabeth Street Garden to let in the brisk night air and dropped the courier bag on the chair. Lifting out the laptop, she plugged in the projector and opened the screen. The bright image cast on the wall over the mattress mirrored her inbox. The NCMEC email remained unopened.

She turned, took the few steps to the counter, and opened the box. She wasn't hungry, but it was a routine to eat Prince Street when she came here for sleepovers. Not a rule. More a routine. Routines kept everything feeling normal and logical. Especially when everything was absolutely abnormal and illogical.

The pizza was the perfect melt of browned cheese and pepperoni. There was just enough burnt edge. She lifted up a slice and took the tip in a small bite. It had exactly the right crunch and slight hint of char. Ten out of ten. They knew her at Prince Street. She always ordered her pizza extra crisp — an extra five minutes in the oven, please. She chewed intentionally. Two hundred and eighty-five calories in a single slice of pizza. Just a number. A nice, logical, unemotional number.

The glowing image on the wall over the bed burned a hole in her back.

She placed the slice on a plate and took a long sip of Pepsi. Not a Diet Pepsi because all the fake stuff was bad for you. Just a straight-up, sugar-filled Pepsi. One hundred and fifty calories. A nice, cold fact.

Just a few more bites, Mila. Get something in your stomach.

She robotically chewed four more bites and set the remaining half slice back in the box.

Finally, she walked to the chair, sat down, and took a deep breath before opening the NMEC email. On the wall, the cover letter read, *"Although a valuable tool, we are aware that the initial viewing of this new image may be difficult for you and other family members. You may want to consider having a close family member or friend present when viewing the image for the first time."*

Adrenaline shot through her chest. She didn't have any family members. *Breathe, breathe. Ten, nine, eight.*

The letter continued. *"This image won't be added to the missing child's poster for ten days while we garner law enforcement approval."*

Seven, six, five—

She double-clicked on the attachment.

Seventeen-year-old Jimmy splashed across the wall in full color. He looked real. The image looked like a photograph, not a drawing.

She jolted backward against the chair as if hit with a heavy object.

He had big, blue eyes, similar to their mother's, curtained by long lashes. Flat but high eyebrows ran across either side of a smooth forehead.

Oh, Jimmy. She exhaled.

Her gaze dropped to his nose. This year, it was larger, more adult. More manly with less fat. His lips were thinner than she remembered, and his cheeks were sunken. The cowlick over his left eye was pronounced.

Tears stung threateningly in the back of her eyes.

In the image, Jimmy wore a plaid, red-and-blue shirt over thin shoulders. A full shadow of tight facial hair covered his lower face.

She stood, turned, and strode to the counter. Her fingers

rested on the smooth surface. She began to tap. *Right, left, right, left.*

The NCMEC artist, Archer Robinson, who had recreated Jimmy the last four times was talented, but the likenesses never expressed emotions. No matter how much this process brought back colorful, palpable memories of her younger brother, it also delivered a grim, jangling sense of lifelessness.

She leaned over, took another deep breath. Fingers tapped. *Right, left, right, left.*

She turned back to the glowing image and let the sense of this adult man, a half-stranger, press around her. A seventeen-year-old man — with stubble — was her new reality. *Seventeen Jimmy.* This was her Seventeen Jimmy.

Ten minutes later, Mila rang a number stored in her phone.

A male voice picked up. "Archer."

"Hi, Archer. It's Mila Pascale. Sorry. Sorry it's late."

"Hi, Mila. Don't be sorry. I was expecting your call. How're you doing today?" The question was a tribe thing. A sad, tragic tribe. They all knew that nobody in the tribe ever truly had a good day. They had better days and worse days. A good week, a bad month.

She replied, "OK."

"I hear you. Thinking about you."

"Thanks."

"How are the classes this semester?" He knew about her FBI aspirations.

"Progressing."

"You'll get there. I have faith."

She said, "Thanks."

He waited.

She stared at the glowing image on the wall. "He has a five o'clock shadow."

"Yes." Archer paused. "We do that." He spoke slowly, as if preparing her for the worst. "We make certain assumptions when we're working. Not all humans, of course, are the same. And we don't know what their daily habits look like. They could be very tidy, for example. Or they could be quite messy. You know, maybe they don't brush their teeth as much as they should, like the rest of us." He was trying to insert some lightness into their conversation.

It wasn't working. The attempt was a three out of ten, really. She waited.

"What we've seen with seventeen-year-old males with difficult pasts is that they're often not living in the most stable situations. They may not have the ability to wash and shave every day."

She stared at Seventeen Jimmy.

Archer continued. "We make an estimate, that males of a certain age may have, as you've rightly noticed, a five o'clock shadow."

She exhaled. "I don't think he will."

He said very softly, "OK."

"Can you do me a second one?"

"Yes, of course. But maybe…"

She closed her eyes.

"I know we've talked about this in the past, and you only sent the one photo of Jimmy's father. Is there any way you could find another? Perhaps a more recent photo of the father?"

The photo Archer had of her father was from long ago. It had been taken before Jimmy had been born. Her father sat beaming, white teeth under almond eyes. Her mother, pale skinned, sat next to him holding a two-year-old Mila dressed in a pink dress. Her father had moved back to Brazil right when James had been born and Mila had been four. Her mother never spoke kindly of him. Called him a rat. A sneaky rat who cheated, ate cheese that wasn't his. Mila said softly, "I'll try."

"If you can. No pressure, Mila, no pressure."

"I'll try."

His voice was tender. "OK, Mila. That would be helpful. You call me if you find anything."

A few minutes later, she closed the image of Seventeen Jimmy. She didn't want to look at Archer's image with the stubble anymore. Next, she typed in an internet search for *João da Silva*. The results were huge. Apparently, both his first and family names were extremely popular in Brazil. She narrowed the search for New York City and surroundings. The results were still considerable. Who knew there were so many João da Silvas in the world?

Her fingers tingled. Her mother hadn't said much about him, other than he'd immigrated to New York at the age of fifteen while working on a ship.

She typed in a search for Brazilian shipping companies. There were nine.

She combined the first shipping company name with João da Silva. Nothing. She repeated with the second shipping company. Nothing. On the third attempt, a result pinged. A João da Silva worked at Pacifica, but the image she found of him was an unsmiling man in his sixties. Seventeen years ago, her father would have been in his early twenties, so now he would in his early forties. The man in the image was too old.

She typed in the fourth shipping company name, *N.E.T.*, and *João da Silva*. The link to one result flashed on the screen. She clicked it.

Staring from her laptop screen was Jimmy's smile, two prominent rabbit teeth and almond-shaped eyes.

She shot up from the chair and moved back from the smiling face. Anger coursed through her. Maybe if he had been in their lives, Jimmy would have still been here. She pointed a finger at the screen, but she had no words. There were not enough words in any language to describe the blame and anguish attached to a father who had left his children.

She slid back into the armchair, snapped a screen shot, and sent it as an attachment to Archer.

He replied immediately. *"Got it. I'll send you an updated image in a few hours. Mila, just know this will delay when the image goes up on the missing poster a bit. We have to get law enforcement approval."*

She leaned the back of her head against the armchair and stared at the ceiling.

Tears streamed.

She whispered, "I'm still here, Jimmy. It's OK that you're grown up. I'm still looking. I still love you. I'm going to find you."

Chapter Four

Dom took notice of Ladybug and the boy as they exited the plane from Los Angeles. The slender, attractive Black woman was still wearing her black ski jacket and was holding the hand of the boy in a Mickey Mouse tracksuit. He looked tired but walked diligently alongside her. The red arm of the boy's puffer jacket extruded from her big purse like a snake head. In her other hand, she pulled a small roller that moved smoothly behind. Her movements were not urgent as she kept pace with the crowd progressing the concourse of Terminal B toward the main building and the AirTrain. Her husband wasn't due to land in Terminal C for another hour and a half.

Dom fell in line thirty feet behind. No need to stay too close and risk being detected. She knew where they were headed. She texted Cape, "*On our way to you.*"

In the main concourse, Ladybug paused to read the arrivals board. The young boy held her hand uncomplaining.

After a quick ride on the AirTrain, Ladybug, the boy, and Dom arrived in Terminal C. Ladybug led the boy into Abruzzo ItalianRestaurant at the main lobby of Terminal C to kill some time. They were shown to a table in the back.

Dom passed the restaurant and took up position near a wall of windows with line of sight into the eatery. She texted Cape, *"Holding Terminal C lobby as they eat."*

Over the tarmac, the sky was blue. It was crisp for the end of October and would get colder soon. She didn't mind the seasons changing. It was nice to have things to look forward to like the holidays. This year, she and Beecher had Mila to add to their Thanksgiving dinner. She'd have to think up some vegetarian recipes for Beecher's latest diet. What did vegetarians eat instead of turkey? She would invite Lea if she was staying in town. That meant getting a sticky pecan pie from the specialty store in the neighborhood. Lea loved over-sweet Southern desserts. And maybe she'd invite Owen. Her heart thumped.

Oh, no, you don't, Agent. She pushed the thought from her mind. There was no time for that sort of nonsense on an operation. A CI operation, for crying out loud.

Her phone buzzed with a text from Lea. *"How's it going?"*

She responded, *"Slow. Surveillance."*

"I have an update."

Dom slipped in an earbud and called her. "Tell me."

Lea said, "We have something on Ice Pick."

The Ice Pick case was their longest-running investigation. For four years, they'd been in pursuit of an elusive cyber stalker who lured young boys with a very specific profile: aged eight through ten, white, small, with a mobility disability. He had been involved in the cases of six missing boys so far. They had dubbed him "Ice Pick" because he used a variety of computer hacks — the first one they identified was called "Black Ice Slice" — to get the boys' phone numbers via their parents' phone company accounts. Ice Pick would send texts to the victims pretending to be their parents. His actions weren't brilliant. Murderers didn't deserve compliments. But they *were* looking for someone with a cold, calculating, and patient mind who was able to manage any number of moving pieces, not least of which was the use of a different hack for each crime.

Lea continued. "I heard from Quantico. I'll know the specifics within the hour. Hopefully. They said they'll be sending it soon. I'm watching my inbox like a hooker watches for her pimp. You know, like not in a good way. More like I can't not watch that corner cause he just found out some of his meth was stolen and he thinks it was me and *oh, lord here he comes*. That kind of way. Obviously, I will call you as soon as I hear."

Four years. Six boys. This was the first possible break in two years. It was a big deal.

They sat silently on the line for a few minutes. It was something they did often during stakeouts.

Lea broke the silence. "I looked up our Wakanda man. He hasn't been in the US in eleven years. Guy is very careful. I'm surprised he's risking this trip—"

"You're not—"

"Relax. I didn't dig into our own files. He's got a Red Notice, Interpol. I tracked it down from there. Your dude lives on the border between Namibia and the Kalahari in South Africa. This is his second wife and the boy is his only known child. I'm sending you all their names via text."

The phone vibrated and she glanced at the text. "*Thato Khosa, 43 yrs, 5'10", Amahale Khosa, 36 yrs, 5'9", Bandile Khosa, 5 yrs.*"

Dom wondered if Amahale had known her husband

was an arms trafficker when she'd agreed to marry him. Did it matter? So many women didn't have good choices.

Lea asked, "When's the last time you saw Owen?" She meant FBI Agent Owen Whyte.

Dom's heart rate spiked. *Those blue eyes. Those shoulders. That unusually innocent grin on a grown man. That crazy engaging laugh.* "Nice change of subject."

"We're doing surveillance. There are no conversational rules. Am I right? So. Talking about Owen. When was the last time you actually set eyes on his fine self?"

Dom mumbled, "Two weeks ago."

"Why?"

"Why what?"

Lea snarked, "You know exactly what I'm asking, Miss Sass. Why so long ago?"

"We're both busy."

"No, you ain't. We're in between. We're working cold cases."

"He's busy."

"No, he ain't. He's still on medical leave."

Dom clamped her lips. She never won when Lea was in a mood. Which was often.

Lea said quietly, "It's the Velk case, isn't it?"

Dom's chest clenched. Dartanian Velk was currently LAPD Head of Internal Affairs and formerly NYPD's Head of Internal Affairs. He was also responsible for the death of Dom's father. Based on the recent snooping done by Dom and the misfit team of Lea, Mila, and Owen, the Bureau had opened an investigation and the suspecting Velk had wisely gone quiet, choosing to lie low, remain in his job, and play chicken with the FBI.

Lea repeated her question. "It's Velk, isn't it?"

When Owen Whyte returned from his medical leave, he was to be assigned to the case.

Why was Lea always so smart? It *was* the Velk investigation that was coming between them.

The case could take months and an enormous effort to make it prosecutable. The US District Attorney of New York was not going to take the case to trial if they didn't have enough to convict. An investigation of such a high-profile public figure would require an extraordinary level of diligence: nailing the evidence, chasing the leads, solidifying the witnesses, and cleaning the documents. In order to keep her sanity and to not contaminate the investigation, Dom needed to stay far clear of the work. But she also needed Lady Justice get to the heart of the matter, vindicate her father, and send Velk to jail.

If Owen was working the case, Dom wasn't sure how she could not ask him questions. Further, how could he not respond? She blinked against the harsh airport light. "Yes, it is the Velk case."

Lea asked, "So it's *you* who's putting off seeing him? Have I got that right?"

"Yes."

"Has he been asking you out?"

Damn her. "Yes."

They had been on three official dates. The first had been to a movie. A thriller. He'd taken her hand over the armrest and her heart had nearly exploded. But after, they'd agreed a movie wasn't a great first date. The second date had been a dinner. They'd gone to a nice place near his apartment. She had been exhilarated and nervous that the location meant they might end up in bed. But he had been the one who had said over dessert, "I think we should take this a bit slow. Like mature adults."

Her chest clenched. *Was that a blow off?*

He had said immediately, "Because I am pretty sure this could turn into something serious."

Warmth had spread across her heart.

The third date, she had taken them cart racing. It had been a huge success. True to their pact, they had ended the night with only a kiss. A deep, thrilling kiss. But only a kiss.

Lea interrupted her thoughts. "Why you being so coy with our hottie boy Owen? Have I taught you nothing about the mating rituals of normal people? You two are young-blooded and ready for action. Why not just get your chiseled bodies between the sheets already?"

Dom closed her eyes against the image of Owen naked and aroused. A tingle crawled up her jaw.

Lea asked, "Tell me this: How many times has he chased you since the carting thing?"

The phone burned in her hand. There were at least five messages over the last seven days from him. Each one trying to get them together. "A few."

"Exactly how many?"

"Five."

"So pretty much every other day, he's texting?"

"Yes."

"Asking you out?"

"Yes."

"Have you responded at all?"

"I respond to him."

"But you're not agreeing to see him?"

"I mean, I'm ... conflicted."

"Miss Sass, we are all conflicted. Life is a fractious constellation of clarity and confusion through which we careen. You make the most of what you've got in the moment. Behold, I will do a new thing, / Now it shall spring forth; / Shall you not know it? / I will even make a road in the wilderness / And rivers in the desert."

"Are you quoting the Bible and comparing my love life to rivers in the desert?"

"Isaiah 43:18-19. And let's be clear. Not your current love life. Your *potential* love life. At the moment, there are no rivers. Like nothing flowing at all. Also, do not question King James. You can't really put the genie back in the bottle now that you two have admitted you like each other."

Dom clamped shut her lips.

Lea pushed. "You know you can't date someone if you don't see them, right?"

"We're not dating."

"Lord help me, I have never met someone so stubborn."

"We're not dating."

There was a long pause across the phone. "Two wary solo travelers trying to find trust. It's like you both have your bags packed and you haven't even checked into the room yet."

Bags packed. Wary solo travelers. It was exactly the right image. Why was Lea so smart? Dom took a deep breath. "It's just hard. I want to ask him about the case. But I know I can't. It all feels weird. Strained."

Lea's voice softened. "I hear that."

"Isn't there advice about not dating someone where you work?"

"Sure. Don't shit where you eat?"

"Exactly."

"It happens all the time."

"Does it?"

"Sure. Where do you think adults meet other adults? Listen, eventually, you two are going to have to whack Willy Wonka into Wonderland."

Her heart raced again. The exhilaration was terrifying. To distract her nerves, she said, "That's not a legitimate phrase."

"Sure, it is. And when you finally do hump that fine ass, honey, it's gonna be hawt."

She ignored the lump in her throat. "Dating a fellow agent is so cliché. So tacky."

"Nobody has to know."

Dom scoffed. "Yeah, right."

"You have a point. All of Javitz will know. So, to that point, you might as well jump in headfirst. Let the shiz hit the fan. Beat them to the punch."

"That's a lot of metaphors."

"Indeed, my fine hesitant friend."

Dom relented. "OK, OK, I'll get back to him."

"Thank the sweet baby Jesus."

Ladybug and Bandile appeared in the entrance of the restaurant and Dom said, "I gotta go."

Lea hung up.

Ladybug stepped into the river of passengers flowing toward the gates. They moved quickly. Her back was rigid and she kept a tight hold on Bandile. He was tired, his feet slow and heavy. She pulled the boy and the rolling bag.

Dom fell in line behind the pair. *What happens to Bandile if they take the wife?* It was always the children who suffered the most. A fact she knew intimately. She kept twenty feet back, weaving through the crowd as the entourage entered the eastern concourse leading to Gates 71-99.

She texted Cape, *"On the move down East Concourse."*

In her hand, the phone buzzed: Cape was calling. She picked up. "Walker."

He growled. "Where?"

She glanced overhead. "East Terminal. Now near Gate 78."

"No! That's not right. Our guy is arriving West Concourse. Gate 124."

Dom spoke clearly. "Now passing Gate 80. Moving with intent."

"Shit! Stay on her! We're coming to you. Lines open."

Chapter Five

Wafting over the garden, Elizabeth Street noises had softened by midnight. Except for two more missing slices, the pepperoni pizza sat cold in the greasy box. The Pepsi cup, however, was empty and the caffeine was driving Mila's fingers as they flew across the keyboard. The research idea had started with Archer Robinson's mention of the missing posters. The comment had scratched at the back of her mind, like the clicking of a cicada deep in a bush. It had been years since she'd looked at the missing persons posters or the various websites of law enforcement around the country. It was time to dig in again. *Better to keep active, moving forward.*

Her search had begun with the New York State active missing persons page. Images and descriptions of New York's missing persons were organized into three categories: children, college, and vulnerable adults. She clicked through to the children section and scrolled down to James Pascale. The unfeeling eyes from Fifteen Jimmy, updated by Archer two years ago, stared back and her fingers paused.

How many children were still listed as missing from New York?

She began scrolling and counting, past the image of a young Black girl around the age of six, with braids and pink bows: *Dina Steton, Bronx, missing 2019.* Past a fat little white baby with lots of red hair: *Laura Dansby, Brooklyn, missing 2018.* Past a Hispanic boy with unruly hair: *Pedro Marco, Manhattan, missing 2012.* Reaching the bottom of the page, Mila whispered, "118." There were 118 active cases for children gone missing in New York.

She clicked the tab for college-aged young adults and began scrolling. Nine. There were nine active cases for New York.

She moved on to the page for vulnerable adults. 32. There were thirty-two active cases in New York for vulnerable adults.

Overall, there were one hundred fifty-nine active missing persons for the state, of which 74.21% were children. It was a disproportionate amount. But it made sense. It was easy to grab a child. Easy to hide them away.

She rubbed her eyes. *Keep moving. Don't sit around waiting for Archer's updated image.*

On her screen, she opened up a new Excel spreadsheet. Toggling between it and the website, she began to copy the data and photos for each of New York's missing persons. It took ten minutes to copy the adults, five minutes for the college students, and twenty-five minutes for the children.

She started a new column and tagged each person's ethnicity based on the photos. Next, she added columns for eye color and hair color. She was on a roll. Columns for sex, current age, and age gone missing were filled in. In two final columns she inputted where they had lived and from where they had been kidnapped.

She sat back and examined the spreadsheet. The data was soothing. Cold, unemotional facts. But did it say anything? Were there any discernable trends? Perhaps nothing singular in New York, but what about compared to other states? What about East Coast versus West Coast?

Forward motion.

She clicked over to the similar page for New Jersey. Ninety-two open cases.

Standing, she moved briskly to the kitchen counter, where she started the kettle for instant coffee. It was going to be a long night cleaning the data of active missing persons cases across all fifty states.

At four A.M., Mila texted Lea Peck. *"You available?"*

Lea was calling within a minute. "Mila, you OK?"

"Yes, I'm fine."

Lea exhaled. "Jesus, Mary, and Joseph. You gave my poor Southern heart quite a stir-up. Child, what on earth are you texting me about at four in the morning?" Her voice was calm and soothing, despite the hour. It was a characteristic of all the staff at the Bureau.

Mila said, "I think I've found something."

"Good Lord. This couldn't wait, oh, I dunno, maybe two hours till sunrise?"

She didn't feel bad. This was too important. "I have found an anomaly in some data I'm looking at."

"Back up. What data?"

Sound normal. She needed to bring Lea along with her from the beginning of the hunt to her recent discovery. "I scrubbed and cleaned data from each state's active missing persons cases."

Lea stayed silent. This was a sensitive subject.

Mila pressed on. "I included and coded all data available on the state pages. Then I focused on the children."

"OK?"

"On ethnicity-based factors, there was no discernible pattern, other than the overall finding minorities are missing at more significant rates than whites."

Lea *hmph*ed. "I bet."

"For age, nationwide, the most common age of a missing child is six. Then I went back and coded for the size of the population where they disappeared, town versus medium city versus large city."

"You did that manually?"

Mila ignored the question. The answer wasn't important. What was important was that Lea understand the ultimate finding. "There was no real discernible pattern based on location."

"I may not like doing it, but I am in my bed with my phone to my ear and I'm listening."

"Then I looked at age. Of the open cases for missing persons across states, the percentage of children remains fairly consistent at seventy-five percent. More kids go missing than adults."

"Yes."

"Girls outnumber boys two to one."

Lea rustled in her bed. "I'm listening."

"Then I found something. Wyoming's numbers are off. Very off. Their stats of girls to boys are opposite the national average. It's twice as many boys than girls missing in Wyoming."

"OK. But maybe it has something to do with Wyoming only having half a million people, as the least populated state—"

"I factored that in. I compared Wyoming against the other low-population areas of Vermont, D.C., and Alaska. Only Wyoming has an anomaly."

"What about closed cases? Maybe Wyoming is better at closing cases."

And there it was. Mila exhaled. "I don't have access to closed cases. I only have data from open cases listed on law enforcement sites."

The phone line was silent for a long moment before Lea said slowly, "You want to compare your anomaly to the Bureau's National Crime Information Center database."

The database housed all open and closed missing persons cases across the country. If Wyoming's anomaly was based on the fact that they had closed statically much higher cases, Mila would be able to prove that. "It's the closed cases I don't have line of sight on."

Lea whistled.

Mila said softly, "Running the same queries on the Bureau database is the only way to make sure."

There was another long pause. "What exact data do you need?"

"Sex, age, date missing, location. I don't need ethnicity."

Lea's voice softened. "Miss Mila, honey. Wyoming is a long way from New York."

She meant that this research would not likely turn up anything about Jimmy. Mila said, "I know."

"Is this a healthy pursuit for you?"

Lea was always frank. Some would surely think *too* frank. But for Mila, it was refreshing. Lea was smart and quick, so whatever she was thinking was sound. Pit bulls were fearless and intentional. "I'm just going to run this down. Then I'll let it go."

"OK, honey. Yes, I'll check the data for you. I'll have it by later today, most likely." Lea hung up.

Chapter Six

Up ahead, Ladybug had picked up Bandile and slung him on her hip, moving at a quick clip, the roller bag zipping behind. Dom glanced over her shoulder. Fifty feet back down the concourse, three men in plain clothes were weaving through the crowd in pursuit. She recognized the tallest with the dark mustache as Peter Cape. He was followed by a shorter Hispanic agent with black hair and a bald, average-height Black man. Two of the original five-man team had stayed at the W's original arrival gate, just in case.

She spoke into the earbud. "You're in my sight. I'm passing Gate 85."

At Gate 86, Ladybug paused to set Bandile down. She leaned in close and kissed his head.

Dom halted and turned to the window. "Paused."

The three agents slowed their approach.

Ladybug smoothed Bandile's face with her right hand. She hefted the purse back up on her shoulder.

Bandile must be extremely tired, Dom thought.

As Ladybug straightened, she tilted her head, paused, and turned to look down the concourse.

Dom twisted sideways and froze, a bored traveler gazing out the window. "She's scouting."

The three agents slipstreamed behind moving travelers.

In the window's reflection, Dom saw Ladybug scan the crowd, face by face, as if something had alerted her to a trail. Or maybe, as she was closing in on her husband's arrival, she realized she hadn't checked if she was being followed.

Outside the window, big, fluffy clouds drifted against a blue sky. A huge United airplane taxied to a gate. On the black tarmac, a baggage truck waited patiently, towing four empty trailers.

Ladybug picked up Bandile's hand, tapped it against her thigh, turned, and resumed her march to the far gates.

Dom spun to follow. "Clear. She's moving."

When Ladybug reached the second-to-last gate in the concourse, Gate 96, she pulled to a stop and stood the roller by her side.

This is it. This must have been the husband's arrival gate. Cape's information about his original gate was incorrect.

Dom retreated to Gate 95 and held her position.

Behind her near Gate 92, the three agents pulled up slowly, spaced apart.

Cape's voice was slow and calm. "Walker, fall back to Gate 88. You're eyes only. Gomez, back to 91, Harper stay at 92. I'll stay on her."

If this was the site of the rendezvous between Ladybug and the target, the family would retreat back down the concourse to baggage claim and the airport exit.

Gomez and Harper took their positions.

Dom moved slowly to Gate 88 and sat in a chair among a crowd waiting to board. Cape had moved in position near the bathrooms across from Gate 96.

The door to Gate 96 opened as an airport worker in a green vest pushed through. He was followed by a gate attendant in a blue uniform.

Within three minutes, passengers began disembarking in a single-file line. The first was a well-dressed couple in their seventies followed by a young man in jeans and a long, woolen coat. The next passenger was a businesswoman in a trench coat with a suit underneath. The next to exit was an olive-skinned man about thirty in jeans and a white shirt followed by a Black woman Dom guessed to be about sixty-five years old. A tall, Black man swept through the doorframe.

Dom stiffened. *Is this W?*

Ladybug glanced up, catching the Black man's eye over the crowd. She swept the boy up in her arms, facing him away from the target, and hugged him to her chest, keeping him from seeing his father.

Confirmed. This is W.

W turned and strode down the concourse.

Cape whispered to the agents, "Eyes on. Let her follow. Then take staggered formation."

W passed Cape and the two other agents before Ladybug set the boy down, grasped the roller suitcase's handle, and followed in pursuit.

The agents fell in line behind Ladybug, keeping a distance of twenty feet.

Dom stood and followed.

What happens to Bandile if they take the wife? The boy was too young to process the trauma that would be inflicted if

As Ladybug straightened, she tilted her head, paused, and turned to look down the concourse.

Dom twisted sideways and froze, a bored traveler gazing out the window. "She's scouting."

The three agents slipstreamed behind moving travelers.

In the window's reflection, Dom saw Ladybug scan the crowd, face by face, as if something had alerted her to a trail. Or maybe, as she was closing in on her husband's arrival, she realized she hadn't checked if she was being followed.

Outside the window, big, fluffy clouds drifted against a blue sky. A huge United airplane taxied to a gate. On the black tarmac, a baggage truck waited patiently, towing four empty trailers.

Ladybug picked up Bandile's hand, tapped it against her thigh, turned, and resumed her march to the far gates.

Dom spun to follow. "Clear. She's moving."

When Ladybug reached the second-to-last gate in the concourse, Gate 96, she pulled to a stop and stood the roller by her side.

This is it. This must have been the husband's arrival gate. Cape's information about his original gate was incorrect.

Dom retreated to Gate 95 and held her position.

Behind her near Gate 92, the three agents pulled up slowly, spaced apart.

Cape's voice was slow and calm. "Walker, fall back to Gate 88. You're eyes only. Gomez, back to 91, Harper stay at 92. I'll stay on her."

If this was the site of the rendezvous between Ladybug and the target, the family would retreat back down the concourse to baggage claim and the airport exit.

Gomez and Harper took their positions.

Dom moved slowly to Gate 88 and sat in a chair among a crowd waiting to board. Cape had moved in position near the bathrooms across from Gate 96.

The door to Gate 96 opened as an airport worker in a green vest pushed through. He was followed by a gate attendant in a blue uniform.

Within three minutes, passengers began disembarking in a single-file line. The first was a well-dressed couple in their seventies followed by a young man in jeans and a long, woolen coat. The next passenger was a businesswoman in a trench coat with a suit underneath. The next to exit was an olive-skinned man about thirty in jeans and a white shirt followed by a Black woman Dom guessed to be about sixty-five years old. A tall, Black man swept through the doorframe.

Dom stiffened. *Is this W?*

Ladybug glanced up, catching the Black man's eye over the crowd. She swept the boy up in her arms, facing him away from the target, and hugged him to her chest, keeping him from seeing his father.

Confirmed. This is W.

W turned and strode down the concourse.

Cape whispered to the agents, "Eyes on. Let her follow. Then take staggered formation."

W passed Cape and the two other agents before Ladybug set the boy down, grasped the roller suitcase's handle, and followed in pursuit.

The agents fell in line behind Ladybug, keeping a distance of twenty feet.

Dom stood and followed.

What happens to Bandile if they take the wife? The boy was too young to process the trauma that would be inflicted if he was pulled savagely from both his parents in a public place. *There had to be a better way.*

Fifteen minutes later, the entourage entered the cavernous baggage claim area. It was a cacophony of commotion: people spoke loudly on phones; parents yelled at kids; and teenagers laughed and joked. Outside, taxis honked and police officers whistled at the traffic.

W checked the board for his arriving bags and moved calmly to Belt 10.

Ladybug made her way past Belt 10 before circling back to face her husband over the carousel. Their eyes met only once.

Cape stopped five feet behind W.

Gomez and Harper moved in twenty feet behind in a pincer formation.

Dom circled the carousel and stood five feet behind Ladybug and Bandile.

W scanned the faces in the crowd.

Cape whispered, "We take him on my count. Cuffs last resort. We want this arrest as quiet as possible. Copy?"

What happens to Bandile if they take the wife?

Gomez and Harper said in unison, "Copy."

Cape said, "Walker, you move *after* me. If she stays quiet, she can get in the transport with us. The boy can come too. Otherwise, cuff her immediately and she goes in separate transport."

Uh-oh. "In the separated scenario, what about the boy?"

"The boy goes with you. There's a backup transport in parking lot."

Please, no. She had a better way. She opened her mouth to protest.

The belt on the carousel stuttered into movement and a loud beep clanged.

Cape growled, "Go time," and stepped to W's back.

Dom strode around Ladybug and knelt before Bandile, eye to eye.

Chapter Seven

Ladybug stiffened.

Behind Dom, the first suitcase tumbled onto the conveyor belt with a huge bang.

This is the better way. Dom held out a hand to the boy. "Hello, Bandile. My name is Domini. It's nice to meet you."

Bandile took her hand, staring at her.

Ladybug yanked Bandile close, but Dom held his hand tightly to keep him in place and looked up into Ladybug's wide eyes. "I'm FBI."

In shock, Ladybug waited.

Dom spoke over the chaos of the room. "I'm here to help you and Bandile."

The boy tried to retract his hand, but Dom held his elbow. She was in charge.

Ladybug glanced frantically across the carousel toward her husband.

Dom instructed, "Look at me."

Ladybug slowly returned her gaze.

"They are taking your husband. Now. There is nothing

you can do. The one thing you *must* do is protect Bandile. Are you hearing me?"

Ladybug blinked.

"I have a deal for you. It will save Bandile from an awful fate. If you make a scene, you and your husband and your boy will all go away in separate cars. You will be separated. Indefinitely. Do you understand me?"

The boy started again to pull against Dom's clasp. She moved to hold his shoulders and said to him, "I am speaking to your mother. You will be calm, Bandile."

The boy stilled.

Dom looked back at Ladybug. "Instead, if you go *quietly* with me, outside, I will keep you and your family together."

Eyes wide, Ladybug sized her up.

Dom insisted, "Tell me you accept this deal."

Ladybug relented and nodded.

Dom rose, keeping Bandile's hand in hers.

Across the space, the three agents were walking W to the door.

Cape said in her ear, "Transport. Now. Nice and smooth to the curb. Walker, keep her five feet behind."

Dom nodded Ladybug toward the exit. "Come with me now."

They turned and headed for the exit door, just your average passengers leaving an airport.

Back in the Lancia, Dom rubbed her eyes as she rang Lea.

Lea answered with a gentle voice. "I'm here."

"It's over."

"And?"

"They all left together. As a family."

"Well, that's something, Dom."

"I guess. It's something."

They both knew the wife and the boy were in for a long struggle with law enforcement and immigration. When they got sent back to South Africa, they'd face even more procedures. Maybe Bandile would settle into a normal life somewhere and his memory of this night would fade. Maybe he would be resilient.

On a higher floor, a car revved. Dom hung her head, taking in a deep breath. While the dark mojo of this operation didn't cut as deep as their own, it still lingered, weighty in her chest.

Lea asked quietly, "You OK?"

Two lanes over, headlights beamed as a car started up. She took another deep breath and lifted her head. "Yeah, I'll be OK."

Lea said, "I heard from the lab."

Dom blinked and her mind cleared. "Go."

"Ice Pick's latest hack had an identifying code. The lab guy says they're pretty sure it's a fingerprint of only one hacker in the world."

"Pretty sure?"

"They can't say with one-hundred-percent certainty. They gave it eighty-percent certainty. It has all the key coding identifiers of one guy."

"Who is he?"

"He's bland. That's what he is. Intentionally, incredibly bland. Thirty-six years old. White. Born Michigan. Single. Registered voter as Independent. Busted when he was twenty-four for hacking into his local bank and transferring ten thousand bucks. Served twelve months. Since then, his programs have popped on their radar a few times. He codes worms. Burrowing types. But he sells the programs, doesn't actually insert them himself. They haven't been able to bust him because he doesn't do the crime. His name is Brad Johnson. I told you he was bland. On paper, he runs a cybersecurity firm called 'Vanilla Orchid.' Get this — he has a website with just a photo of an orchid."

In the dark car, Dom shook her head.

"Well, of course I looked that up. 'Cause me. Turns out in the real world, the vanilla orchid actually attaches to a tree, more like using the tree as a foundation. It absorbs moisture from the air. Doesn't harm the host tree. A real parasite."

"Selling worm programs to his clients that he doesn't actually execute. Keeps his hands clean."

Lea said, "I mean, looks like he learned from his hard time in the slammer. Stay out of trouble. He lives in a five-million-dollar home in a part of Vegas called Summit Club. Go bland. Go vanilla. Literally living by that motto."

"Ice Pick bought this guy's worms."

"Exactly. That's the hypothesis."

"Which means vanilla Brad Johnson may know our guy."

"Exactly."

"Call the Vegas field office. See if you can track down someone who knows about Vanilla Johnson."

Lea replied, "On it."

"Nice work. I'm on my way." Dom turned the key in the ignition and the sports car growled to life.

Chapter Eight

A ray of morning sun warmed Mila's face, disrupting her sleep. In her dream, she was staring at Seventeen Jimmy from ten feet, mute and in a state of disbelief. Neither said a word. The silence grew oppressive. Was he angry that she had never come for him? Would he yell at her? Or would he give her the cold shoulder he had perfected as a child whenever he'd been embarrassed? He wouldn't attack her, would he? As part of her independent studies, she'd taken three courses in self-defense: one based on Jiu-Jitsu, one on Situation Effective Protection System Women's Self-Defense, and one on de-escalation and conflict resolution. Would she need to fend off Seventeen Jimmy? Or maybe he wouldn't recognize her, having jettisoned the soft memories of an older sister to survive the brutality of a kidnapper?

Through the vapors of the dream, her stomach knotted painfully, and her cheek burned.

Her eyes blinked open. The disquiet lingered in her gut. She turned on her side to glance at her laptop screen. It was nine A.M. At least she had gotten some sleep.

Last night, after speaking with Lea, she had gone for a walk around the block to slow the mental spinning. She'd had too many Pepsis and her anxiety had been on overdrive. During the walk, she had thought of another possible line of inquiry. Once Archer returned the revised Seventeen Jimmy, she would do an internet image search, identifying similar-looking young men and then digging into their details. The new plan had soothed her restlessness enough that she'd returned to the apartment and crawled in bed.

Now, she reached and tapped open the inbox. Archer's email sat at the top. *"Revised."*

She took a deep breath, pushed up, and straightened her back against the bare wall.

In a wave, the dream returned. Seventeen Jimmy's eyes were so blue, they were piercing. Should she be the one to break the silence? Yes, she should speak first because she had tracked him down. But what to say? Should she suggest they go get coffee? Or something to eat? Young Jimmy had loved ice cream, pies, and fudge. Maybe Seventeen Jimmy preferred a salty breakfast? Eggs and toast? What an odd thing to think. But there were no right or wrong answers in this situation. Finding your missing brother after seven years was a completely unique and terrifying situation.

The dream lifted slowly, reluctant to leave.

She took a deep breath and clicked open the attachment.

Seventeen Jimmy version 2.0 popped on the screen. The blond hair, the cowlick, the bigger nose. But this time, the eyes were slightly different, more almond-shaped, like João da Silva's. The five o'clock shadow was gone. He looked less depressed, more optimistic. Maybe Seventeen Jimmy didn't like ice cream anymore. Maybe he preferred lemon meringue pie.

She set the laptop on the wood floor and pressed up from the bed.

Better get that kettle going again. Coffee was just what she needed.

The image search turned up twenty pages — over a hundred linked results — of young men with blond hair, blue eyes, and thin lips.

It was a good start.

She clicked open the first image. The photo had been taken in front of a Ferris wheel at a beach amusement park and was one of a dozen on a shared photo app. She clicked through, head cocked, staring into the young man's eyes. It just didn't feel like Jimmy. She clicked back out.

It was going to be a lot of manual work digging into this many photos. She took a slug of coffee.

She began discarding at a quick pace, opening images, scanning for the almond eye shape and the cowlick. She would back out of any image where the basics didn't match. It was a blur of young males, many of them smiling. None with the two big teeth.

Thirty-six minutes later, she lifted her fingers off the keyboard.

Almond-blue eyes stared at her under dirty-blond hair. There wasn't a cowlick, but the nose was similar to Archer's rendition. The chin felt right.

She opened the accompanying site. The photo was part of a collection of a small college soccer club in Ohio. The image was of Spencer Johnson, the captain. Soccer. Jimmy had played soccer. She clicked through pictures of the team on the field, at practice, lined up in rows for an official image. Spencer smiled widely, with broad shoulders and a good dose of confidence. Had her Jimmy continued to play soccer with his new family? She stared at the broad shoulders and thin legs of Spencer. No. This wasn't Jimmy. Something about Spencer didn't feel familiar. He was really tall. Too tall. No one in their family was that tall.

She sighed, clicked out of the site, and stretched. Time for another coffee.

Forty-five minutes later, another image startled her and her fingers hovered over the keypad. Slowly, she tapped the mouse pad to zoom into the image and leaned toward the screen. The blue eyes were familiar. A bright light banked off the corneas. The nose was strong and the lips matched her memory. The face was set against a black background like an artistic portrait.

She clicked on the accompanying website link to a subsite of www.maxfieldclafoutis.com. The portrait was one in a series. The next image was an older woman with deep wrinkles. Then a young baby with fat legs and chunky arms. A pale man in a hospital bed pleaded with the photographer.

She returned to the image of the young, blond man. It was a gut instinct, a feeling, but this felt very similar to what she imagined Jimmy looked like now. Dirty-blond hair. Almond-shaped eyes.

Had she found a clue to Jimmy online? The odds were one in a million. Maybe more.

She clicked to the main home page of the artist. The white font of a quote filled a sleek, black page.

"Maxfield Clafoutis. A contemporary artist who succeeds in boundary-pushing and experimentation like no other. His exhibits yank by the throat, forcing you to confront the subject with wide eyes and bated breath. He is a visionary, a true genius." - Art in America

She'd never heard of him. And if you pressed her, she wouldn't be able to explain contemporary art. She looked up the definition.

"Contemporary art is a loose term, as there is no cohesive vision or material. Artists in this genre work with varying subjects, materials, and methods. It is heterogeneous and diversified. Many contemporary artists experiment with style and statement, often pushing the boundaries of 'what is art.' It is not unusual for contemporary artists to produce work that reflects current events or hot topics. Often the focus of the artwork is on the audience, less on the actual piece of art."

She pulled up the Wikipedia page for Maxfield Clafoutis and skimmed the entry.

"Maxfield Clafoutis (born November 2, 1946, died October 2020) was an American contemporary artist. Born in Oxford, England, he moved with his family to New York at a young age. He is recognized for searing critiques of corporate greed and the wide use of artistic medium, including video, print, photographs, and installations."

She scrolled lower into the references. Most people didn't check footnotes. It was a huge oversight.

The fifth source cited was a five-year-old article written by a Lennox Lewis that had appeared in *The New Yorker* titled, "A Study of Longevity in Art: Clafoutis's Durability."

The New Yorker article opened on her screen with two images. The first was of an older man sitting on a neon-green sofa in a large, loft-like space with three walls made up entirely of books. She zoomed in on the photo and stared at the artist's face. He looked kind but jaded. The smaller, second image was of a series of portraits similar to the one that had enticed her down this rabbit hole.

The article spoke of his creative process. What inspired him? How did he choose mediums? It felt like a puff piece before a big exhibit. There wasn't much in the article about his personal life. In fact, there was nothing about him except that he resided in Brooklyn and was a mercurial, quiet, and very much private artist.

She returned to the smaller article photo of the portrait series. There was the older woman with wrinkles. There was the chubby baby. But there were also two new images. One of a farmer hunched over dry barren soil, staring up wide-eyed at the photographer.

The last image stole her breath. Another young blond man, this one a teen in a white T-shirt, stared with blue eyes at the camera. A tuft of hair stood up from his forehead in a pronounced cowlick.

She swallowed. *What were the odds that this was Jimmy?* One in a billion? It was a super long shot.

She tapped out a quick search for Lennox Lewis.

Bingo. Lewis was a freelance journalist based in New York who had gotten a journalism degree from NYU.

Mila's phone vibrated with an incoming call from Lea Peck.

She opened the line.

"Hi, Mila. I was able to track down the numbers from Wyoming. I think you may have actually identified something. There are too many missing boys in the Wyoming cases over time. You were right. Twice as many boys missing as girls, which is the opposite of the national average."

Mila whispered, "Where are the boys?"

"I don't know. I'll send you the data, but your finding was correct."

Clafoutis's portrait of the blond boy with the cowlick stared at her. "I might have another lead."

"OK, you stay in touch with me, Miss Mila. If you find something, you call me first. Then I will call Dom. In that order. You to me, me to Dom. You don't go off on some merry little goose chase on your own."

"Yes."

"We clear?"

"Yes."

"Because I don't want you in trouble again. You can be a dangerous little brainiac if left to your own devices. You need some guidance and some goddamned guardrails. Say you agree. Say the word."

So frank. So true. Bright-blue eyes stared at her. "Agreed."

Part II

Part II

Chapter Nine

Riverton, Wyoming uniformed patrol officer Monnie Friday sat down in front of Dakota Thunder and smiled. His mother said he was eight years old, but his birth certificate said nine. Even for an eight-year-old, he was small, let alone a nine-year-old. In the cool interior of the small house, he wore only a T-shirt over an old pair of jeans, and his ribs were visible. His certificate also said his native name was Hiisiis Hokecii or "Little Sun."

Monnie's own parents had moved from Wind River to Cheyenne when she'd been eleven. She considered herself fortunate. "Dakota, I'm glad you're back."

Dakota was lucky. There was another boy, Anton Norris, Yéíy Níitóuu or "Hollering Otter," from a different part of the rez who had gone missing four weeks ago and hadn't returned. Eight years old. Long, black hair and thin shoulders. At this point in the case, the assumption among the Riverton Police was that Anton was dead.

Dark Northern Arapaho eyes that mirrored her own

glanced at her sidearm then back to her face. As a rez kid, he showed no fear. He'd seen too much.

At sixty miles across and fifty miles long, Wind River Indian Reservation was the seventh-largest American Indian reservation. It was home to 3,900 Eastern Shoshone and 8,600 Northern Arapahoe and all the issues that accompanied America's reservations: low employment, low income, substance abuse, poor educational opportunities, and plenty of domestic abuse.

From the corner of the cold living room, Dakota's mother, Mama, said, "Yes. Yes. Scary stuff out there. We hear all the things."

Monnie asked, "Dakota, I'm going to ask you some questions, OK? You answer what you want. You do not have to answer everything. Just what you want. I may be a police officer, but I'm a nice one and I am not demanding anything you're not comfortable doing. Does that sound OK?"

He nodded stoically.

"You've been gone two days. Do you know where you were those days?"

"Off the rez."

"Do you know where you were?"

Dakota shook his head.

"Did you go alone?"

From the corner, Mama watched his back.

He didn't blink. "I went into town with Paul. In his car."

Mama grumbled, "You weren't supposed to go with Paul."

Monnie looked up and in the same gentle voice, "It's OK, Mama. We're just glad to have him back, right?"

Mama stuck out her chin. "Riverton Police's not doing enough about our boys gone missing."

"We're doing all we can."

"You haven't found the other."

"That's true."

"So you're not doing enough."

"We are following all our leads."

"You ain't got no leads. And they put a junior officer on the case. Not a senior officer."

Monnie Friday had been with the Riverton Police only two years. She'd been a policewoman for three. After her first year in the Cheyenne police force, she'd asked for a transfer. What Mama had said was true. She raised an eyebrow to concede the point.

Mama grumbled, "They put young lady Arapahoe officer on this for lots of reasons. Mostly, they don't care."

Monnie squared her shoulders. "Mama, the entire force is working this case." That was not exactly accurate. With no leads on Anton Norris, the case had gone quiet. Very quiet.

Mama grunted. But she leaned back against the cinder block wall.

Monnie pulled out a small, spiral notebook and resumed her questioning of Dakota. "OK, so you went into town with Paul. Then what?"

He wiggled his hands. "He left. Didn't come back. For hours."

"Paul left you in the car and stayed away a long time?"

"Yes."

"Do you know where you were parked?"

He nodded. "In the lot of the 789 Casino."

It was a dodgy, smoke-filled, slots-only casino out on Route 789.

Mama cleared her throat.

Monnie asked Dakota, "And then what?"

"He was gone hours. It was getting dark. I decided to walk into town."

A small kid walking along Route 789 at night and no one had picked him up. Shame on Riverton. It was a common refrain. "Good. Very good. Keep telling me your story."

"I was hungry. I stopped at the diner. I went inside. The waitress was nice. She asked me if I wanted something to eat. I said *yes*. She put me around the corner. At the counter. Near the kitchen door. Got me some food. Mashed potatoes. Turkey. It was night."

Monnie would speak with the waitress at the Mountain View Diner. "And then?"

"The waitress asked if she could call Mama. I said *yes*."

In the corner, Mama said, "Yes, she called me. I said I didn't have a car to come get him. Waitress said she'd send a patrol."

That jibed with the station logs. A call had come in from the diner, and one of the other officers, Johannsen, had driven over. By the time Johannsen had arrived, Dakota had been gone. She looked back at Dakota. "Why didn't you stay for the officer?"

"The big man came and told me he would take me home."

"What exactly did this big man say?"

"He said Mama had sent him. That I was to go with him. Home."

Little Dakota had just been doing what he'd thought had been expected.

"Please, keep telling me the story as you want to," she said.

"I ate the rest of the turkey. Then went with Big Man to his truck."

"Can you describe Big Man?"

"Old. Gray hair. Big, fat face."

"Can you describe the truck? Do you know what kind of truck it was?"

Dakota shook his head. "It was old. Creaky. Smelly. Had a cover on the flatbed."

"Smelly inside?"

"Yes. Like old truck."

"Creaky?"

"My door creaked when I opened it."

She wrote it down. "Got it. Keep going, Dakota. You're doing great."

"I got in the truck. We drove. It was dark." His face showed the first hint of fear.

"Did you know where he was driving?"

"No. I asked him. But he hit me."

She sat back. "He hit you?"

Dakota nodded. Placed his hand on his cheek.

I will kill this Big Man. But it was just a thought. Monnie was a police officer. Of course she wouldn't kill him. But she'd throw his ass in jail. "OK, we're here now. He won't touch you again."

Dakota stared into the distance for a long moment, no doubt reliving that period in the truck. He whispered, "We drove a long time."

He had been picked up two hundred miles from his home, near Pinedale. "Maybe you fell asleep?"

His eyes were wide with relived fear. "I didn't fall asleep."

This was a tough little guy. She nodded. "Did you ever tell the man your name?"

"No."

"Good. Good. And then?"

"We turned on a dirt road."

"OK?"

"A really long, dirt road. Maybe an hour?"

That *is* a long, dirt road. *Noted.*

"A nice house. A big house. Some lights. The big man took me inside. He went into the kitchen. I heard him open a door, rattled. Like maybe metal? Yeah, metal. I ran."

Wise kid. Rez kid. "Where?"

"I ran out the front door and down the dirt road. I ran hard. He was yelling. There was a flashlight on the road, so I ran off the road into the woods. Scary. But better than his light finding me."

Smart kid. "And then?"

"I climbed up a tree. High."

His eyes were wide.

Monnie said gently, "We're here. You're safe now. What happened?"

"Finally, he stopped yelling. I saw his flashlight go back."

"What did you do?"

"I climbed down. Walked the other way. Walked by the moon. Away from the house."

"How long did you walk?"

"I don't know. I was very hungry. Tired. The sun came up. I found the road. A lady in a red car saw me, pulled over."

Mrs. Thomson. Monnie had already spoken to her. She was the one who'd seen him north of Pinedale and picked him up. "You were very brave."

Mama cried. "And lucky!"

Monnie agreed. "Yes, brave and lucky."

Dakota ended his story. "That lady in the red car drove me back here."

"She's nice. She lives in town. I already spoke to her."

"I thanked her."

Mama interjected. "I thanked her too! I hugged her."

Monnie sat back. "Now, Dakota. I do need some help. Can you tell me what you saw inside that house?"

His eyes widened.

She soothed him. "No, no. This is just in case, some day, I can find that big man so I will know it's him. I will never tell him who you are. He has no idea."

Dakota closed his dark eyes and whispered, "Lights. Fancy lights. High. Very high. Trophy heads. Like the white man likes. Big trophies. Black bear. Mountain lion. Moose. Glass wall. Deck. Lake outside on the other side of the house. No lights on the lake. Just the moon. Mountains."

"Are you sure about the lake, that there were no lights?"

"Very sure."

There were over thirteen hundred lakes in the Wind River Range. "What about anything else about inside?"

"A big statue. Near the stairs. A cowboy. On a horse."

There were probably thousands of statues of cowboys in Wyoming. "Bigger than you?"

He nodded.

"Anything else?"

He opened his eyes. Shook his head. From the corner, Mama grumbled, "It's enough, Officer."

Monnie agreed. She shook Dakota's hand. "Thank you, Dakota. You've helped me a lot. You're a very brave boy."

Outside in the patrol vehicle, she underlined three phrases from her notes: metal door, isolated lake, cowboy statue. It was something.

Chapter Ten

When Lennox Lewis opened the door of the Upper West Side apartment, a waft of lovely perfume filled Mila's nose. Lennox had a long mane of auburn hair that swept off her forehead and cascaded over her shoulders. She smiled brightly with very white teeth. "Mila?"

Mila nodded.

Lennox opened the door wide. "Come on in. You want a coffee or tea?"

Mila shook her head. "No, I'm fine. Thanks."

They settled on opposite ends of a light-pink couch in the sunny living room of a small apartment.

Lennox said, "OK, hit me. You doing some kind of project for school?"

Mila cleared her throat. *Sound normal, not spectrum. Give context.* "I'm digging into some old cases as part of my criminal justice program." *Not entirely a lie.*

Lennox grinned. "Oh, fun. Super. What can I help you with?"

"I was looking into missing children and was doing some internet image searches—"

"Missing kids?"

"Yes."

"Oh. Oh. Dark. Tough. Cool. I'm here for that."

The enthusiasm made Mila squirm. There was nothing *cool* about missing kids. She pressed on. "So, I was doing an image search—"

Lennox's eyes widened and she leaned back dramatically. "Wait. Are you searching for a specific kid who's still missing?"

"Yes. It's a long shot. But yes."

"Oh, God. OK. Right. Hit me."

"I found some similar images in portraits done by Maxfield Clafoutis."

With shocked distaste, Lennox crossed her arms over her chest. "Your long shot has to do with Clafoutis?"

"I saw your profile of him in the New Yorker."

"Well, well, well. Isn't this *interessante*?"

"So, I wonder if you can give me some more...*color* about your interview?"

"Of course." Lennox straightened her shoulders as if bracing for a challenge. "Let me tell you, that guy was not cool. And I'm OK speaking ill of the dead. Since you saw the article, you know that the interview was about three years ago, about a year before he died."

Mila nodded to encourage her.

"*The New Yorker* explicitly wanted me for it. I was young. Recent grad with a dual art history and literature degree with a focus on modern art, so of course we all knew who Clafoutis was. But to be honest, while I was a little stunned they'd called me, I had a feeling I knew why. I hadn't transitioned and was apparently just what they were looking for." She gave Mila a knowing, quick wink.

Had they pimped her? She waited with a blank look for the rest of the story.

Lennox leaned forward and spoke slowly as if to a child. "I. Hadn't. Transitioned. To a woman yet."

Mila nodded. "Yes. I understood that part. I was waiting for you to tell me why that was important for the assignment."

Lennox smiled bemusedly. "I. Love. You. If everyone were so blasé about who people were, this world would be a much, much better place. Anyhoo, it's important because they knew Maxfield liked effeminate boys. I mean, I was young and already girly. I guess I was his type. They do whatever they can in the literary field to get ahead. Don't let the snooty side of things fool you. They're all after the bucks and the fame, baby. So, yes, my agent pitched me to do the story. Clafoutis had probably looked me up before he'd agreed."

Noted. Maxfield was gay and had a type: young and effeminate. Mila prompted her, "You did the interview…"

"Yes, I went over to his Lower East side digs. He was in town rarely, so the timing worked. This huge apartment. With bricks and sunlight and wood floors. An old warehouse. It was sick. Absolutely gorgeous. He sized me up right away. And listen, I know a size up. That man would have jumped me in a heartbeat if I'd given him a sign."

"Did he try anything?"

"Not at first. I held out my card and it set us out on the right foot. I had him sit across from me at this long, wooden table. Like *really* long. Like he had huge picnics at this table. Ran right down the room. So, I sat on one side, took out my computer and pad — I use both. And I had this list of questions."

"Like what?"

"He needed a visibility boost. His last run hadn't been great. So I asked stuff they ask artists. Inspiration. Challenges. The art world. I mean, some of his stuff was really avant-garde. Really revolutionary. Some of it was kinda boring. He had high years and low years. Some of his sculpture was great."

"Not consistent?"

"His stuff always had an emotional tenor to it. That's for sure. But the execution was a bit off sometimes."

"And the interview?"

She pushed her hair off her shoulder. "In most interviews, I get about two hours' worth of usable stuff. Then I distill and use quotes in the article. I had already done a heap of background research on him. I had a lot of that article already written."

"What about personal stuff?"

"Halfway through the interview, he gets up to use the bathroom. When he comes back, he walks right up behind me and puts both hands on my shoulders and, like, caresses my neck."

Mila whispered, "What did you do?"

"I said, 'Mr. Clafoutis, you seem to be mistaken. I have been sent here by the managing editor of *The New Yorker* to conduct this interview. I'll thank you to sit back down so we can finish.' It worked. He huffed his way back around the table."

Mila blinked. She wasn't used to stories of sexual harassment. "Wow."

"Totally."

"Anything else about the interview?"

"I mean, I try to get one or two vulnerabilities to give it some pizzazz, but Clafoutis had been down the interview road a hundred times. He hung around with a ton of movie types. Lots of famous dudes. He knew what I was digging for. He kept up a very good façade. He knew how to keep private. I got nothing of interest out of him."

"Got it." Mila's chest constricted. "So, in the article, the photos. Can you tell me about them?"

"*The New Yorker* photo guy went over about a week after me. Apparently, Clafoutis was getting squirrelly about the interview. Don't know why. Everything I submitted was on the up-and-up. Nothing bad. But I guess they wanted me to choose photos that would make him feel better about the whole thing. So, they sent me a batch. Said to find ones that spoke to the substance of the interview."

Mila opened her phone, flipped to the image she had saved of Clafoutis on his green couch.

"Yeah, I told them to use that one."

Mila showed her the other, smaller image from the article. "I zoomed in on this series on the wall. Do you know when he made them?"

"Oh, the portraits. He was quite famous for those. He took those images and printed them on, like, tissue paper and hung them as thousands of leaves on trees in this one section of Central Park. Thousands of them. It was totally bizarre and quite incredible. Crowds swarmed." Lennox shrugged. "For three days and then it rained and all those tissue leaves disintegrated."

Mila's throat dried. "When was that?"

"Oh, the same year I interviewed him. Three years ago."

Jimmy would have been fourteen. *It could be him.* Her heart raced.

Lennox flagged red fingertips in the air. "Wait, do you think that series has something to do with your cold case?"

She swallowed. "It's a long shot."

Lennox was shaking her head in confusion. Her long, silky hair shuddered. "I mean, how is it a long shot?"

Mila zoomed in on the Jimmy lookalike. "This one, he looks like the person I'm searching for."

Lennox's mouth opened in a big O. "Oh, god."

Mila nodded.

Lennox gave her a side-eye. "Listen, that old goat was creepy. I'm telling you. I mean, who knows what he got up to on his ranch?"

What? "What ranch?"

"His entourage kept it pretty secret. I guess they didn't want him getting stalked outside New York. Like I said, he knew how to keep his shiz private."

The hair on Mila's nape was tingling. "Were you able to track down where his ranch was?"

"I don't know. Out west, for sure."

What were the odds? "Wyoming?"

"I actually don't know. I know it was out west." She screwed up her face. "I don't remember why I think that."

Mila whispered, "How would I find out?"

Lennox thought about it. "I mean, the New Museum on Bowery did a nice exhibit of all his work after he died. And they do keep good research. There may be something in their archives that could help?"

It was a great suggestion. Ten out of ten. The museum was around the corner from her apartment; Mila had explored it many times. "Good idea."

Lennox beamed, evidently proud to be of help. "Oh, oh, I really hope you find your missing kid!"

It's a long shot. One in a trillion. But it's been seven years and I have all the time in the world to chase down long shots. She simply said, "Thanks."

Chapter Eleven

Owen Whyte sank into the thick cushions of the chair in the basement office of Eileen Bremmer, the psychiatrist assigned to him by Employee Assistance Counselor (EAC).

Her unflappable demeanor, more than her smooth, graying hair, reminded him of his mother. "Morning. How you feeling, Owen?"

He shrugged happily. "Good. Good. Better."

Eileen Bremmer specialized in trauma. "Pain levels?"

"I feel pretty good, to be honest. Who would have thought nine weeks was about right for a gunshot to your shoulder?"

"Great. I'm glad to hear that. I think we can agree you're ready to take that fitness-for-duty exam with MORU?" She meant the Medical Operations and Readiness Unit.

"Yeah, I think I'm good."

"You feeling good to get back to work?"

"Absolutely. I'm ready."

"Excellent."

"In fact, they've already assigned me to a new case."

"That sounds interesting."

The Velk case was going to be one of the biggest, most scandalous cases of high-level police corruption in the history of the United States if it bore fruit. The previous Head of Internal Affairs for police departments in New York and Philadelphia, and now Los Angeles was an asset of the Ukrainian Russian organized crime group out of Brighton Beach. Yeah, it didn't top that. "Oh, it's going to be extremely interesting."

"Oh?"

"They've sent me a lot of reading to get up to speed. The expectation is that I should be ready to hit the ground running when I get clearance to go back to work." He smiled ruefully. "It's just, I'm not sure."

"About what?"

"I'm thinking of bowing out. Altogether. Telling them *no*." He glanced out the window, reluctant to admit something.

She waited like a good therapist.

He nodded as he turned back. "It's about Dom."

"Would this case somehow come between you two?"

"I think it already has." He couldn't tell her the details, but he could give her the general outline. He chose his words carefully. "There is always the fear a case like this will go sideways. That there isn't enough to prosecute. Especially around a money trail. I'm good at what I do and we wanted me in there. But we can't talk about it now. If we do, and their side finds out later, at some point in the case, it may be brought into an appeal." He shook his head. "So instead, it's already become this wall between us."

She pressed her fingertips together as if in prayer and

leaned her chin on them, looking over at him with kind eyes.

He grinned reluctantly. "I don't want that wall."

"Huh. Tell me more."

He cracked his neck. "I want us to have a shot at a relationship."

She'd let her hands rest on her lap. So patient, so professionally supportive. "How does it feel to say that?"

He glanced away, then back, grasping for the feeling. "It feels like the truth."

She waited.

He continued with the thought. "I want us to have an opportunity to get to know each other like normal people."

"You want it to be authentic."

"Yes. I want us to get know to each other honestly. Without outside pressures."

"And that doesn't scare you?"

"Exactly. Me just saying that would have, in the past, maybe even a month or two ago, made me scared. Now... not so much."

"What *do* you feel?"

"Optimistic."

"Excited about the possibilities?"

He nodded. "Yeah."

"Good. And good for you for recognizing it. Now what does it mean for you to bow out of the investigation?"

"I need to go in and tell them the conflict of interest may be a problem. There will be questions. But in the end, they will agree with me."

"You'll have to tell them about your budding relationship?"

"I'm not sure. But I would if it came to that."

"Will that affect your career?"

He chewed his lip. "I mean, this case is huge."

"So a missed opportunity?"

"One thousand percent."

"And how do you feel about giving up an opportunity for a personal relationship?"

He shrugged. "It feels right. It feels healthy. It feels objectively mature."

She nodded.

"It feels like a good choice."

"Good. That's all it needs to feel. We only ever make decisions with the information we have at hand."

"Now, I just have to tell Dom."

"It sounds like, from what you've told me about her, that she's pretty levelheaded."

Chapter Twelve

From across Bowery Street, the New Museum of New York was a sight to behold. Seven white metal boxes, each two stories high and of varying dimensions, were stacked in an enormous Dr. Seuss wedding cake. The structure rose dramatically from the mundane surroundings of the Lower East Side, a mix of lighting and restaurant supply stores, juice bars, and gyms.

Mila pushed through the main doors. The first floor exhibit space was a soothing expanse of white walls and polished, gray cement floors, a blank canvas waiting to be filled. A sloped ramp invited visitors to explore all the floors. She flashed her New York University student card to a young woman with a pink mohawk and nose rings who barely glanced up. Nobody ever checked student cards in the city. "I'm hoping to see some images in the archives."

"Sure. Fifth floor. Take the elevator. You'll see the Resource Center when you get there."

The Resource Center was stark white. White desktops. White walls. White floor. Mila slid into one of the tables and wiggled the mouse — the home page sprang across the screen — and chose *"Archives."* She clicked her way through the tabs to *"Artists"* and typed in *Clafoutis*.

Five results appeared on the screen.

An article about New York artists from 1989 in *The New York Times* referenced a Clafoutis exhibit the year earlier as *"illuminating and daring. A masterpiece from an innovative soul."* The *New York Magazine* had run an article titled, "The Guardrails on Art in the 1990s" about a multi-artist exhibit that had run May 12th to August 20th, 2001 at the New Museum. She clicked through and saw that Clafoutis had only one image in the lineup: a tree atop a bright-green hill in a vast, empty plain, wrapped in barbed wire. The image was titled, *Freedom, 1996*. It felt like a progressive political statement about human constructs caging in the organic. Given Mila's working hypothesis, that Clafoutis had taken a portrait of a teen boy — eerily similar to her Jimmy — as the source of his sexual desire, the image felt sinister.

The third search result was simply named *"Clafoutis"* and it was a montage of an exhibit that had appeared in this museum, September 22nd to November 27th, 2018. Two years before he'd passed away. She pressed through the images quickly at first to place herself. It was a composite of all of his work. She returned to the beginning and moved slowly through them. Some were just the full-sized image of artwork. Others were photographs of a wall of art. It showed the artist's evolution. Early in his career, he had produced a number of sculptures. They were almost all done in gray material that appeared to be granite. She wondered how hard it was to chisel away a big granite rock. The exhibit had on display three of his early sculptures, each one a representation of a young man.

She sat back and stared at the three sculptures. All

young teen boys. This Clafoutis inquiry may yet prove to be one hell of a wasted rabbit hole, but boy, did this guy feel creepy.

She returned to the rest of the exhibit. In his thirties, he had moved into multimedia: flat paintings with three-dimensional aspects. Some paintings stuck out into the room, but they were all sized roughly 5' x 5'. The colors were bright reds and vibrant greens. She zoomed in on one image of five vaguely human-looking individuals with balloons as heads — faceless balloons. The piece was titled *Hot Air*.

During his forties, he'd increasingly used photographs as the foundation for huge multimedia pieces, one even taking up the whole side of a three-story building.

His last era, already into his seventies, had been a decade of black-and-white photograph-wrapped installations and she thought of Lennox's description of the installation in Central Park. The last piece of the exhibit was the finished sculpture on loan from MoMA to the New Museum. Mila sat back and crossed her arms, staring at the sculpture. It was a huge hand, knuckles bent, tips of fingers driving into dirt. The wrist was at such an angle as to imply that the person was underneath, as if someone were struggling to pull themselves out of a grave. The title read *Cry for Help*.

In a few of the exhibit photos, Clafoutis appeared at the showings, always surrounded by groups of fans. Many of them were celebrities she recognized. Lennox had been correct. He'd known a lot of famous people.

Her phone pinged. It was a note from Lea. *"Dom wants to hear about the anomaly. Let's meet at Grecco's Diner in two hours."*

She pushed back from the desk and headed to the office door at the end of the room.

The curator librarian was a middle-aged man with a brown ponytail, a thin face, and a pronounced jugular. He looked up. "Yes? Can I help you?"

"My name is Mila."

"Hi, Mila, what can I do for you?"

"I was just looking up some information in your database digital archives. I was an intern until recently over at the Museum of Natural History. Your archives are quite something." *It was the truth.*

He smiled proudly. "Probably one of our top priorities is to be able to provide public access to all of our wonderful artists."

"Well, it's working. I thank you." *Incredibly normal and polite.*

He beamed.

"Do you have additional information that's not in those archives? I'm looking for anything on Maxfield Clafoutis."

"Oh, of course. A contemporary museum without information on Clafoutis couldn't call themselves serious, now could they? And it's really good timing; I was just heading to our library in the basement. I'll get you everything we have on him."

"Super!" *So normal!*

Thirty minutes later, she opened a white cardboard box four inches deep. Folders and papers were stacked neatly. She lifted them out gingerly and set them across the clean, white table and began methodically sifting through them. She was mindful to keep them in their same order.

Most of the documents were more photographs of Clafoutis's art and exhibits.

Toward the bottom of the pile were six 5 x 8 glossy

photographs. She laid them out side by side. The five images had been taken in the same setting: a wide interior of an artist's workshop with bare wood walls, planked wood floors, two huge easels and outsized painted canvases leaning in stacks against the walls. In the first, a middle-aged Clafoutis was walking toward a blank canvas on one of the two easels and the next image was of him standing in front of it. The third was Clafoutis leaning over a rounded statue. In the lower-right corner of the third image, the photographer had cropped someone from the scene. The hem of a denim pantleg appeared in the corner. Mila slid over the fifth photo. It was a wide-angle shot of the studio in which Clafoutis and a male figure with short, blond hair and denim jeans had their backs to the photographer as they looked through a wide window at the prairie.

Mila's neck tingled. She slid slowly over the last photo. This time, both the artist and the blond had turned toward the photographer.

Mila's eyes widened. The blond could have been a teen version of Jimmy.

She pulled out her phone, taking shots of all six photographs so that she could zoom in on them on her screen. Her fingers pinched the images outward, magnifying the details as much as possible. She started scanning each detail in the photos. It was the third photo that held a clue. On a small table in the corner of the room was a coffee mug branded with the logo and name Wort Hotel.

Her fingers moved swiftly to search "Wort Hotel" on the internet.

Wort Hotel, Jackson, Wyoming.

She slowly lifted her head. *My long shot has just gotten shorter.*

Chapter Thirteen

ASIC Fontaine looked up from his desk as Dom's shadow filled his doorframe. He set down a pen. "I heard the Newark op went smoothly."

She shrugged. "Smooth enough."

"Listen, when I don't hear those guys howling about some security breach, it was a smooth op."

She stepped in and stood with her back close to the wall.

"What can I do for you, Agent? I would have thought you'd take the day off."

She shook him off.

"You get any sleep?"

"Sure." It was a standard Bureau response that was never based on facts.

He held out his hands. "So, what can I do for you?"

"We've got something on the Ice Pick case."

"Oh?" He didn't bother asking if she'd already briefed Barry Lowenstein. Fontaine was too big a fish to care about putting Lowenstein's nose out of whack.

She said, "The labs may have identified the programmer who wrote the latest hack he used."

He leaned back in his chair.

"The hacker lives in Vegas."

He nodded. "Interesting. You check with—"

"Grouse." Andrew Grouse was the Special Agent in Charge in Vegas. "I know Grouse pretty well. I worked with him on Saint Christopher." It was the case that had taken a year to crack. A child trafficking ring. She told him that Grouse had confirmed Vegas was a hub for cybersecurity firms. "He knows of the hacker but never had any reason to engage."

"You want to go out and give your hacker a visit?"

"Exactly."

"What else are you working on now?" Again, he hadn't asked about Lowenstein.

She rattled off the other closed cases they were poking.

He shrugged. "Nothing timebound?"

"No. Nothing timebound."

He nodded, picked up his pen, and resumed reading. "Sounds good to me." It was his approval and a dismissal. It's what she had wanted. Lowenstein wouldn't override Fontaine.

But it wasn't the only thing she wanted. She glanced out the window.

Her hesitation made him glance up. Her stony face made him set the pen down again. "You staying away from Velk?" Fontaine was well-known for being emotionally astute. It intimidated a lot of the male agents.

She held his gaze. "Yes, sir."

He nodded over at his credenza, where colorful binders stood in three stacks. "See those?"

She glanced over. "Yes."

"Those are all the investigations I'm keeping a personal eye on."

"OK?"

"They're color-coded."

The closest, tallest stack was made up of roughly twenty green folders.

He continued. "The green are coming home soon. Grand juries are happening. Bureau is basically just cleaning out the final kinks. While the prosecutors are running the show, I stay in close contact with them. It's part of my job."

The red stack in the middle was the smallest with about ten folders.

"The red are about to be green. Final interviews, confirming testimonies. Shoring up witnesses. Bureau teams can largely be shifted off soon. If a case has too many holes, I'll pull it soon. Obviously in coordination with DOJ, but I, still at this final stage, have authority to pull. They are still with the Bureau, technically."

The black pile had five folders. She glanced back to him.

He raised his eyebrows. "Those black folders are personal. I don't pay close attention to them while they're in early investigation stages. You know the drill, a year, two, maybe more. I'll get some briefings, I'll read updates, but I won't work with the team or get inside the ring." He shrugged. "No need for my eyes on surveillance, chasing leads, witnesses. None of that. And anyway, there are far too many cases for me to get that close."

She watched him.

"But the cases in those black folders are personal to me."

She held her breath.

He sat forward. "All you need to know, Walker, is that the Velk investigation is one of those black folders. It will stay in that pile so I can keep an eye on it."

She ached to know what secrets that folder held and had so many questions. Had they approached the Filthy Five cops? Were they thinking of flipping Gessen? Were there wire taps? Were they closer to identifying the Ukrainian mob that held Velk by the balls? Instead, she nodded slowly.

Hopefully, once Owen came back from medical leave, she'd get some inkling of the investigation's status. She wouldn't ask Owen directly. There would be nothing in writing between them about the case, no texts, no emails. But surely, he'd drop some hints. Surely, he'd let her know there was progress. Surely, they could navigate the sensitivities around his participation in the case.

Fontaine said solemnly. "It's moving."

"OK."

"Oh, and we've got eyes on the cops. They're not getting anywhere near your little friend."

Mila. She exhaled. "OK."

"Agent?"

"Yes, sir?"

"One more thing. I just heard Special Agent Owen Whyte has asked his supervisor to be transferred off the investigation when he comes back from medical leave."

The wind left her chest. *Owen hasn't said a word.*

"Whyte said he had a conflict of interest and that he was too biased based on the work he and your team did." He eyed her. "That he could not remain impartial."

Her jaw tightened.

"We are thankful for his candidness."

She swallowed.

"It was the right decision. I was concerned that there

may be a spoilage issue, what with whatever is going on with you two."

She opened her mouth to protest, but he interrupted with a palm. "Now I don't have to worry about that. It was the right decision on his part."

She stepped from the wall to go.

"You hear me?"

She rolled her shoulders. He was right, of course, but the betrayal stung deep. "Yes."

"Good. Good luck in Vegas."

Chapter Fourteen

Grecco's Diner was three blocks from the Javitz Building in Lower Manhattan. Through the windows, the sun was setting over the west side of the island, casting long shadows through the skyscrapers along the checkerboard streets. Inside, the restaurant smelled of cheeseburgers and French fries. The waitress arrived with three coffees, three ice waters, a plate of biscuits, and a small bowl of butter slabs.

Mila reached for a coffee. Lea transferred a biscuit and a butter slab to her plate.

Dom took a sip of the coffee. It was tart and strong. Not bad. She said to them both, "OK, hit me."

Mila pulled up Archer's rendition of Seventeen Jimmy's image on her phone and slid it across the table. "This is Jimmy. Age extrapolated by NCMEC. This year. It was his birthday yesterday."

Lea stopped chewing.

She spoke softly. "I'm sorry. We're here for you."

Mila continued. "It goes live on their site soon and is

being sent to law enforcement. The last two years, we didn't get any new tips."

She and Lea waited.

"I decided this year to do some digging." Mila explained how she had searched public information and cleaned the data.

Lea picked up the story. "She called me about this Wyoming anomaly, so I pulled all cases, closed and open, of victims under sixteen. But Miss Mila was correct. Wyoming's numbers are off. Too many boys."

Mila added, "Twice as many boys as girls."

Dom smoothed her placemat as she took in the implication. If the aberration wasn't a mistake, it was unpleasant. Extremely unpleasant. "Maybe their data was entered into the system incorrectly?"

Lea nodded slowly. "I actually pulled and manually scanned each file. They are correct, at least in terms of sex."

Whoa. Had Mila stumbled across a pedophile ring targeting boys in Wyoming? Dom stretched her shoulders and took another slurp of coffee.

Mila said, "I also did some more research."

Lea crossed her arms over her chest. "This is why we're here. Dom, I told her we had to loop you in."

Mila continued. "I took that aged image of Jimmy and ran an internet image search." She explained the eerily similar image that was part of Maxfield Clafoutis's work. "Then I saw this." She pulled up the image from the studio of Clafoutis and the denim-clad teen and slid it across the table.

Dom and Lea leaned in. The teen in the photo was a replica of the NCMEC image of Jimmy.

Next to her, Lea whispered, "I'll be damned. Saints alive."

Taking back the phone, Mila swept to the third photo and held it up. "That mug is from Wort Hotel in Jackson, Wyoming."

Dom placed flat palms on the table. "Nice work, kid."

Mila nodded.

She recapped, "OK, a strikingly similar image of a teen, an artist who leans toward teen boys, a ranch studio we think in Wyoming, maybe near Jackson, and very off numbers out of Wyoming. I'm not saying it's something solid, but I am saying it's very hinky."

Next to her, Lea said, "Absolutely."

She said to Mila, "That you chased down this artist, that was a really good investigative move."

Lea nodded.

Mila whispered, "I have time."

She insisted, "But you also followed your gut. That's a huge piece of being a detective."

Lea nodded. "Instinct. Dom's mantra."

Mila looked to Dom. "Is that true?"

"For sure. I've pursued some odd leads, tenuous at best. This type of work isn't linear. Sometimes zigzags lead you to a new discovery."

Mila asked, "How do you know that your instinct is right?"

Dom sat back, thinking about an answer. "It's like a tickle on the back of your brain. Or a whisper that crosses right in front of your eyes, but you can't really focus on it. Sometimes it can be the use of a single word in a way that's off. An internal antenna quivers. Very much like you did with that photo from the portrait. But you have to take that pause, that beat, and listen, really listen. Sometimes it slips away, like trying to grasp smoke. But it almost always comes back." She smiled. "Lots of times, it comes back in the shower or right when I'm trying to fall asleep. You have to let your mind chew on it. Anyway, that's how I've learned to trust my instincts."

Lea said, "If you call out for insight and raise your voice for understanding. Amen." She wagged a finger jokingly. "Proverbs 2:3, if you must know."

Dom shook her head in respectful jest.

Mila remained serious. "Instinctively, I'm not sure there *is* a direct connect between Jimmy and Clafoutis. But that teen in the photo could be Jimmy's doppelganger. I find that very interesting."

Lea nodded. "Me too."

Dom tapped her fingertips. "Me too. And from a Bureau point of view, the irregular numbers are enough to dig in."

Lea said approvingly, "Our girl Mila does not quit."

Dom agreed. "No, she sure does not."

Lea pulled out her phone and searched something, then looked over at Dom. "There are direct flights between Vegas and Jackson Hole."

Dom gave Mila a small smile. "As it turns out, we have a lead in Vegas. I can make a stop in Jackson on my way back home."

Mila sat back with a big sigh.

Dom responded to her relief. "Let's do a little digging, shall we?"

Mila smiled.

Lea jumped in to lighten the mood. "Wyoming. Who would have thunk it? Lots of empty gorgeous landscapes and mountains and prairies. Like, *real* empty. Real big. One could even say that territory is sweeping. And cowboys." She gave them eyes. "And I ain't talking Black cowboys, neither. We're talking west of Mississippi. There's only one

Black cowboy who matters out there. Bass Reeves, am I right?"

Who? Mila turned to Lea.

Lea cocked her head and narrowed her eyes. "Bass Reeves? The famous first Black Deputy U.S. Marshal west of the Mississippi River?"

Dom shook her head.

Mila shook her head.

Lea scowled. "He made a record three thousand arrests. Never once got shot? Most likely inspired the Jamie Foxx character in *Django*?"

Silence around the table.

Lea dropped her mouth open. "You *do* know *Django Unchained*, right?"

Dom and Mila shook their heads.

Lea threw her hands up. "Lord Almighty in the Great Heavens Above, help us with the folks who don't follow American culture. Like any. Like living in a pure, white bubble, you two. Anyway, my point is that's some huge expanse of white cowboy America out there, Wyoming is."

Mila turned to Dom. "I appreciate you doing this."

Dom winked at her. "It's a good start."

Lea laughed. "Mila's a fucking anomaly."

Dom said to Mila, "But keep digging. We're gonna need something a bit more narrow than all of Wyoming if we're going to put any manpower into this. Jackson is one town in a huge state." She blank-eyed Lea. "A sweeping, huge state."

Mila nodded. "Yes."

Lea laughed. "Oh, look at her. She's got the scent like a bloodhound. A little agent in training, this one."

Dom said to Mila with a gentle face, "Mila, just know that my side trip does not an investigation make."

Mila nodded. "Yes."

Chapter Fifteen

The evening coffee crowd in the basement of Javitz was particularly heavy right after dinner around seven P.M. Everybody still working needed a jolt to work the late hours. Lea poured herself a deep cup from the dispenser marked *Extra Strong*. From over her shoulder, she heard, "Lea Peck, how the hell are you?"

She turned to see Special Agent Whyte. Lord, he was a fine specimen. She gave him a smooth, sexy purr. "Whyte, you fine thang. How you doing?"

He laughed at her tone. "Good, good, SOS Peck. How are you?"

Over her cup, she gave him a wink. "Nice to see you."

He laughed again.

"You back?"

"I'm just getting some catch-up reading. My therapist has signed off. So tomorrow I'm headed in to the testing team to dot the *I*s and cross the *T*s."

"How's the shoulder hole?"

He rolled it. "Good."

"That was quick."

"Yeah, right? How are you?"

"I cannot complain. Although this will be my third coffee today. Not a good sign."

"How's the caseload for you guys?"

"And by 'you guys,' in the plural, I assume you're asking about Walker and myself?"

He grinned. "Exactly what I'm asking about."

"Yeah, there's some stuff rumbling."

"I saw Mila downstairs just now."

Her two hands poised the cup in midair as she squinted. "Oh, yeah?

"I just saw her on my way into the building."

"She may be part of that rumbling."

"She told me."

Lea leaned back to get a good look at his face. *He was serious.* She clicked her cheek. "Miss Mila. Miss Mila. What did she tell you?"

"About some connect between a famous New York artist and her missing younger brother."

Lea corrected him. "*Possible* connection. But not probable."

"And Clafoutis's second home out in Wyoming."

She shook her head.

"It's not a Bureau investigation, right?"

Lea cocked her head. "Oooh, Miss Mila is a smart one."

He shrugged. "No reason not to tell me about it."

She shook her head. "I suppose not."

They shuffled along in the slow-moving line together, sipping their coffees.

He said, "And the Wyoming piece is interesting."

She gave him a side-eye. "Oh yeah?"

"Wyoming is the biggest tax haven in America and one of the leading tax havens in the world."

"Seriously?"

"There's been big money moving in there since 2016. Millionaires and billionaires. Wealth management firms call it the Cowboy Cocktail — a mix of some of the most stringent privacy laws coupled with lawyers, estate planners, and agents putting together private companies with hidden ownership."

"The forensic accountant comes up big again. Damn, I did not know that."

He had a twinkle in his eye.

"Don't do it, Agent."

He said to the cashier, "I've got both of us." He looked at Lea as he handed the cashier his card. "It's not a Bureau thing."

"Oh, shitballs, you're going to do it."

"It's about Mila. And her brother."

"Oh, shitballs, shitballs, Miss Dom is not going to like this."

His grin was devious. "It's an interesting investigation."

Brave guy. Lea whistled as she shook her head.

He nodded. "The old crew is getting back together!"

Miss Dom is definitely not going to like this.

Part III

Chapter Sixteen

Officer Monnie Friday had called ahead to the Wyoming Indian Elementary School in Ethete and Principal Beth Whitaker, a curvy blond woman with a wide smile, met her at the top of the stairs with a warm handshake. "How do you do, Officer?"

"Good, good. Thanks."

Whitaker said, "We heard about Anton Norris." Anton was the boy from another elementary school who had gone missing. "We're praying for his return."

Children's laughter rippled across the nearby playground.

Monnie replied, "Yes."

"Do you have any leads on Anton?"

The sad truth was they didn't. They'd interviewed his entire family and set of friends. He had gone missing on his walk home from school. There were no videos, no cell phone information, no witnesses. It was as if Anton Norris had been lifted by a UFO off the middle of a street. She shook her head. "Unfortunately, we do not have a lot to go on."

Whitaker clicked her cheek. "Shame."

"Yes."

"Well, of course, we're all very happy nothing bad happened to Dakota. But it does make us wonder…"

Chief Kantore had not acknowledged that they may have had a serial kidnapper on their hands. There just wasn't enough tying the two boys together. Monnie interrupted Whitaker's musings. "Thank you for seeing me."

Whitaker led her into the administrative office near the school's front doors and nodded to one of the staff. The walls were a colorful collage to kids: paintings, photos, drawings. The room smelled of old-school copy machine fluid and cold medicine. Through internal windows, the squeal of sports shoes on a gymnasium floor was a background melody.

Monnie sat across from the desk.

Whitaker settled in her chair. "What can I tell you?"

"Just a little bit of information about Dakota."

"It must be difficult to do your job and rely solely on a nine-year-old's memory."

"Yes, that's true."

Whitaker noticed someone through the windows and said, "I've asked his teacher, Ms. Dawson, to join us."

The door opened and a young woman joined them. She wore a purple, velour track suit and a purple hair tie. Introductions were made.

Monnie kept the information sparse. No need to add to any possible gossip mill.

Dawson said, "He's a good kid. Has some issues at home. But nothing out of the ordinary here."

"Does he tend to fabricate?"

Dawson shook her head. "No. Not any more than any other boy his age."

"Good imagination?"

She thought about it. "No, I wouldn't say that."

"Good student?"

"He'll be a C or B student if he stays on his current trajectory. No significant learning disabilities. That's what we focus on at this age."

"He appeared small to me."

Whitaker said, "All our students get breakfast and lunch. I've looked up Dakota and he also gets the additional nutritional support program."

"OK, so all-around, a good kid from a low-income single mother family?"

They both nodded.

"And nothing in his files or history here at the school that makes him a standout?"

They both shook their heads.

"Any known trouble with bullying?"

Dawson said, "No, he's really just a normal kid. Given what you've said about the circumstances of his abduction, I'd say he was just at the wrong place at the wrong time."

Later, standing at the top of the stairs in the sun, Monnie had to agree with Dawson. *Wrong place, wrong time.* She needed to dig in on the location of the abduction. Maybe there was a connection to Anton.

Chapter Seventeen

The FBI main office in Las Vegas was a clean, low-slung three-story building on Stella Lake Street. A white, metal fence around the parking lot made a thirty-foot perimeter. This location was the primary office, but the Bureau did have satellite offices in Elko, Reno, and South Lake Tahoe. This office, since 9/11, had been focused on counterterrorism and intelligence, but she knew that organized crime, especially the long tentacles of the mafia, wormed their way through the city. Casinos were an excellent laundry machine for dirty money. Even at six in the morning, the parking lot was half full and Dom wondered how many of them had been working night shifts aligned to the casinos.

On the plane from JFK, she had read through the Ice Pick file again, hoping for any insights on code used in the hacking programs. None had magically appeared. She'd have to wing it with the hacker.

Closing the file, she'd let her mind wander. Owen's silence about his decision to step away from the Velk case still stung. She wasn't sure what she would say to him when they eventually did speak. The text from Lea she'd gotten when she'd landed had been another surprise. *"I bumped into your Owen. He already talked to Mila. He's doing some digging on the Jimmy case. Just to let you know."*

A memory from their second date had flooded her mind. As they'd entered the restaurant for dinner, he'd opened a door and stood aside to let her pass.

She'd laughed. "OK, that's gotta stop. The old-school charm is impressive, but as two law enforcement officers, I think we've moved past that."

He had half-bowed. "As you wish."

The quote from *The Princess Bride*, even in jest, had made her pause. Everybody knew the movie reference. *Was Owen suggesting that he would do whatever it took to make her love him?* Her brain had stumbled, and a blush had burned up from her neck across her cheeks.

He had leaned in close, almost touching foreheads. "Can I get you a drink?"

Even now, sitting in the rented Chrysler sedan, she blushed.

Later, at the end of the night, he'd pulled his motorbike to the front of her house.

She'd swung a leg over, slipped off the helmet, and dangled it by her side.

He'd rested his own helmet on his thigh. "You got a full day tomorrow?"

"A lot. How about you?"

He'd grinned, his white teeth bright. "Oh, you know, more recuperating." Earlier, he'd told her about his sessions with the Employee Assistance Counselor and the upcoming fitness exam.

"I'm glad you're healing."

"Me too."

"I'm sorry—"

"We're done with that whole conversation, OK? You saved my life."

She'd stammered, "You wouldn't have—"

"It was what it was. I'm fine. You're fine. No need to rehash how that situation came about. We're done." He'd grinned.

He's right. "You're right."

"And we need to make some memories that don't involve hideous murderers and gunshots so our conversations are more interesting."

She'd smiled.

He'd said softly, "Tonight was great."

She'd nodded. "It was."

"Like, *really* great."

Her heart had pounded in her chest. *Why am I so nervous? Why is this all so easy and perfect? Why is he so hot?*

He'd taken her hand. "Shall we do it again?"

Her mouth had gone dry. "Yes, let's do it again."

And he'd repeated the movie line. "As you wish."

Oh, god this is happening.

He'd gently pulled her toward him.

The kiss had been strong and gentle at first, but it had soon spiked, deep and hungry.

They'd finally pulled apart, breathless, and he'd smoothed hair off her brow as if he couldn't yet let her go. "I'll talk to you tomorrow."

In the Chrysler, she broke from the daydream. She wasn't mad he'd recused himself from the Velk case. She was just sore that he hadn't told her his plans. It felt like a betrayal. No. It *was* a betrayal. It made her question their intimacy.

She gathered her bag and slipped from the car. *Why do*

relationships have to be so complicated?

Sun streamed in through the windows of the corner office belonging to Special Agent in Charge Andrew Grouse, which overlooked the parking lot. The room temperature was easily sixty-five degrees and chilly. Grouse was a small, sinewy man with a tight buzz haircut. He spoke in clipped sound bites. "This hacker. Brad Johnson. Tell me."

She filled him in on the connection between the Vegas hacker and the program used by Ice Pick.

Grouse frowned. "Shit. OK. Your plan?"

"I'm just going to go have a chat. See where that leads."

"My guys have him on CCTV."

"Oh, yeah?"

He wrestled his mouse to pull up a video on his screen. The scene was a crowded convention center with modern booths with screens, high resolution images, and impressive lighting. "That's Def Con. World's biggest conference for hackers." The image switched to a similar conference hall. "Black Hat. Cybersecurity event. We've IDed him at both." He zoomed in on a still image of a blond man in a black top and white yoga pants chatting with a suited male in a booth. "That's him in the white pants. It's not much."

"Thanks for that."

He leaned back. "We've got good tech out here. Good access too. We work hard with casinos."

"I guess it says something that he's not otherwise on your radar."

"True. He's keeping his nose clean."

"Thanks for that. I'll let you know if it leads anywhere."

"We're here if you need manpower."

She pulled up her bag, readying to rise. "One more thing. I'm going to head over to Jackson Hole after. I've got something I'm interested in chasing down. Unofficial."

"Oh, yeah? You need any help?"

"Maybe I could meet with your guy out there?"

"Sure. I'll call ahead. Roy Cross. He's different. Loner. But he's solid."

And just like that, she'd crossed the Bureau *T*s and dotted the Bureau *I*s.

Chapter Eighteen

The best way Owen knew how to help Mila's Wyoming search was with a two-pronged approach. Neither line of attack guaranteed success, but both were worth exploring.

He had set himself up at his dining room table with a view over the Hudson River. Circling the laptop were the printer, his phone, a landline, a poster board, a calculator, a burner cell phone, and a cup of pens. He rubbed his hands together and clapped. "Let the games begin."

The first line of forensic accounting attack would be to work from the outside inward. He dubbed the campaign Zero In. He would identify all the owners of residences in the Wyoming and with each new piece of evidence, he would exclude possibilities and narrow the pool. It would be an arduous process, but it could provide some interesting data alter that could feed into the investigation.

He set his fingers on the keyboard. Kickoff question: How many homes in Wyoming? Answer: 274,371. The search for Mila's brother was likely to lead to a location outside a major city. Second question: What are the five most populated cities in the state? Answer: Cheyenne, Casper, Gillette, Laramie, and Rock Springs. Working swiftly with the calculator, he deducted the estimated numbers of homes in the five cities — 210,000 individuals — from the state total. Question: How many homes remain in our pool? Answer: 63,000. He blew out his checks. While he'd done searches that had started with a lot more — that number was peanuts compared to New York State's almost twenty million — it would still require the manual download of all records for each of these properties.

He reached for his phone and dialed a number down in Javitz's basement.

A male answered, "Tech. This is Jaimie."

He'd worked with Jaimie Spencer on a previous case a few years ago. "Oh, hi, Jaimie, it's Owen Whyte."

"Hi, Owen."

"I've got a question for you."

"Shoot."

"I need to download all the property records of homes in Wyoming excluding cities and get them into a database that I can manipulate. Location, owner, mortgage, etc. Whatever records are on file."

Jamie whistled, "OK?"

"I'm wondering if there's any way to make that less manual?"

Jamie was thinking it through. "First, I'd have to grab the public lists off each county site. Then I would have to write a script that would pull out the owner's name, the bank info, the location would likely be a street address... Yeah, it's doable. There will be some mistakes."

"That's OK. It's a start."

"Yeah, I can do it."

"You're a hero, Jaimie. Thank you. How long do you think it will take?"

"Dunno. I'm slammed with some other stuff."

"This is not part of an official investigation." He added, "Yet."

"Got it. Maybe I can get it back to you in a week?"

Mila's case was going to take a lot longer than a week to resolve. "Sure."

"Owen, anything you can do to narrow the universe would help."

"Great. Thanks again, Jaimie."

"Sure. I'm on it."

Chapter Nineteen

Mila's bike sped along Central Park's western Bridle Path, past the early morning lookie-loos at Strawberry Fields, the John Lennon memorial, and up past the lake. The park wasn't too crowded this early in the morning. She hadn't been back to the American Museum of Natural History since her internship had ended five months ago and she missed this commute.

She'd been up very early, crawling out of bed at four A.M. to escape the anxiety. Dom's caution that they needed to narrow the focus of their search had been thumping against her brain. The Clafoutis connection was tenuous, but it was all she had.

Armed with a local bakery's largest coffee and a pumpernickel bagel toasted until the ridges were black, she pulled up the photo series from Clafoutis's ranch studio. Munching on the bagel, she zoomed in and out of the photos, examining the view outside the windows: flat land, a limited slice of a mountain — heck, it could even been a hill for as much as was shown in the photo — and some scrubby bush. Was the mountain range enough to triangulate the location?

For two hours, she manually searched images of the three US mountain ranges: the Sierra Nevada, the Appalachian Mountains, and the Rocky Mountains. The Sierra Nevada, running four hundred miles down the center of California, included Lake Tahoe, Yosemite National Park, and Mount Whitney. Most of the images of the Sierra Nevada included snow in the winter, rocky cliffs, heavy trees, and the iconic vista of Bridalveil Fall, streaming from above the valley floor. They did not feel like the range outside Clafoutis's window. The Appalachian Mountains through Tennessee and North Carolina included the Blue Ridge Mountains and the Smoky Mountains and were heavily forested. They also had rolling slopes like waves. The density of the trees in the Clafoutis image were not a match. Finally, the Rocky Mountains from northernmost Western Canada to Albuquerque, New Mexico showed dramatic peaks and valleys. Of the three thousand miles of mountains, there were over a hundred peaks, mostly in Montana, Colorado, and Wyoming. There were just too many peaks for her to manually make a match to the Clafoutis image.

Flummoxed, she stretched her back and rubbed her eyes.

She'd exhausted all the items inside the studio. There was nothing other than the mug that could be used as an identifier.

Outside the windows, there was only scrubby plains and the mountains.

Her mind slowed. Scrubby bush.

She zoomed in on the plants nearest the window. They

were still about fifty feet from the building, but there was good detail in the image.

She slapped closed her laptop and shoved it in her courier bag.

The weather was nice and chilly and the ride through the park was exhilarating. At the path parallel to the 79th Street transverse, she caught a green light on Central Park West and zipped the bike across the pedestrian walk. She needed to move quickly. Her first class was with Professor Mary Chow at eleven A.M. and she didn't want to miss any of it.

She was fortunate to have been accepted for an Individualized Study across the Social Sciences degree. It meant she could take a number of undergrad and graduate classes within the larger theory of criminal justice. Now into her junior year, she no longer even scanned the program descriptions for classes in white collar or commercial areas of the law: contracts, bankruptcy, corporate, arbitration, trade regulation, or some of the more existential topics like labor, environmental, immigration, or intellectual property rights. That stuff definitely didn't intrigue her. Her singular focus was where law met the rubber on the criminal road. What was a crime, how do we convict criminals?

She'd been able to sneak in two classes with Professor Mary Chow. Chow was a professor from a practice with a focus on criminal law and criminal procedure. During the 1990s, she had been an Assistant U.S. Attorney in the U.S. Attorney's Office for the Eastern District of New York, where she had tried cases involving members of crime families. She had also worked in the criminal fraud section of the Department of Justice. She was basically a criminal law badass.

With the individualized study, Mila was also allowed to incorporate some non-NYU courses. Last term, she'd worked with the continuing education team at the Red Cross headquarters building in Hell's Kitchen on West 49th Street to take their advanced courses in Adult and Pediatric First Aid, their automated external defibrillator — or AED — course, and their cardiopulmonary resuscitation — or CPR — course. When she'd passed her last course at the Red Cross, Beecher had whistled. "Mila, if anyone ever gets hurt, you're the one we're gonna want around!"

She pedaled the last stretch down the block on W. 81st and sailed into the underground parking lot of the American Museum of Natural History. The bike squealed to a halt two inches from the bike rack.

The security guard in the hutch looked up. Under a thick head of hair, his big eyes were gentle.

She waved to him. "Hi, Mike."

He pointed a finger at her. "You're supposed to be at school."

"I'm just coming to do some research. Then back to class."

"Good, good. Young things like you need to study so you can go save the planet."

She gave him a thumbs-up and pushed through the *STAFF ONLY* door.

Alexandra Satchen was a botanist with a specialty in conservation biology. She wore bright-red lipstick and dyed her hair a variety of colors, depending on her mood and the month. She had always been very sweet to Mila. Now, she cracked her knuckles as if prepping for a challenge, red fingernails like a matador's cape. Mila's story was engrossing. "Let me see! Let me see!"

Mila slapped down her laptop on Alexandra's desk, flipped open the screen, and pointed at the landscape beyond Clafoutis's window.

Alexandra pulled the laptop closer and zoomed in on the screen. "Oh, yes, yes. I can identify that for you, Mila!"

Mila's heart raced.

Alexandra moved the image in and out, muttering to herself. "Yup, let's see. Numerous slender stems. I'm guessing fifteen centimeters tall. Silvery leaves. Maybe two to five centimeters each. Stem leaves are mostly entire. Basal leaves three lobed." She found a second plant. "Oh, look here. Lucky to have a flower sample. Center flowers. Staminate." She glanced at Mila. "This shouldn't be too hard."

She clicked open a new window and manually flipped through images on the screen until she found one she liked.

Flicking back and forth between the reference guide and Clafoutis's plant, she mumbled, "Yes, yes. Long, narrow, leafy. Spike inflorescence."

She sat back and pointed to the reference on her screen. "This is it. Scientific name is *Artemisia porteri Cronquist*. Of the Family Asteraceae or sunflower. Genus Artemisia has at least fifty species. Otherwise called Porter's Sagebrush."

Porter's Sagebrush. It sounded ominous.

Alexandra's finger scrolled down the screen. "Let's see. Legal status is listed at Sensitive."

Mila asked, "What does that mean?"

"Was going to be listed as Endangered in 1983 but looks like they found an abundant grouping somewhere..."

The blood tingled in Mila's arms.

Alexandra continued to read as she scrolled. "Can be found in sparsely vegetated clay flats, gullies, and depressions. Yes, yes. Here it is! Mostly endemic to the Wind River Basin."

Wind River Basin. Mila exhaled. "Where's that?"

Amanda opened up a new window and typed in Wind River Basin. "Looks like Wind River Basin is big, over 2.25 million acres. Eighty miles of the Continental Divide. In western Wyoming."

Another connection to Wyoming. Dom, we're not in long-shot territory anymore. Mila allowed herself a tight grin.

Alexandra opened a fourth window and pulled up images of Wind River Basin. "Mila, look. The mountains in your image match those in Wind River. Jagged granite formations, alpine forest, open meadows. Lakes and ponds. It's got to be it."

Bingo.

Five minutes later, standing in the hallway, Mila texted Dom and then Lea with the same message. *"The artist's studio was in Wind River Basin. WY."*

Lea responded first. *"Nice work, Miss Mila."*

Dom's reply was quick to follow. *"Nothing conclusive on this artist, but that's a great find. Keep digging."*

Chapter Twenty

Brad Johnson's five-million-dollar home was well-insulated within the golf resort community of Summit Club, only thirty minutes' drive outside the city, but a massive income gap away. The main club building sat in a lush, green bowl of a manicured golf course. The view in one direction was of the Vegas skyline, casinos and high-rises along the Strip. In the other direction, the brown mountains of the Red Rock Canyon National Park rose in a spectacular horizon.

She parked the Chrysler facing the mountains and dialed Barry Lowenstein. This wasn't going to be an easy call.

Lowenstein had been her Supervisory Special Agent for only four weeks, and it was already a difficult relationship. The Bureau had a culture of pay-your-dues, which included being treated badly by superior officers. It was a real traditional system. Most agents just accepted it as a matter of course. Human Resources didn't do much to rein it in. And senior management mostly ignored it. But Lowenstein was different. He was a bully with a mean streak. Despite his character flaws, he had been promoted, which gave him managerial oversight of a six-person team. The power had gone to his head. He was also known within Javitz to have it out for women and minorities. She wasn't sure if it was pure racism and sexism, or if it was some variant of 'they're stealing my job,' but either way, it was abusive.

A week ago, in a team meeting, agents and support staff had been taking turns providing case updates. When it had come to her turn, Dom had said, "We're on cold cases waiting for the next live one." She'd rattled off the name of each case.

Lowenstein had pointed at Lea and barked, "Anything from you, little lady?"

Dom had quickly replied for her. "Sir, I'd prefer you use her correct title. SOS Lea Peck is a respected member of this team."

The room had stilled. You could have heard a pin drop.

Lowenstein had stared at Dom, sizing up her grit. A moment later, he'd chuckled darkly. "You don't say, Walker? I think we all know SOS Lea Peck is a respected firecracker."

Heads had swiveled between Lowenstein and Dom.

She'd risen slowly. "Sir, I'm asking you to deal with your staff with the respect they deserve. 'Little lady' and 'firecracker' are not terms of respect."

Around the room, eyes had widened.

Lowenstein's eyes had narrowed. "Sit down, Walker."

Heads had whipped back.

She'd remained standing. "Sir, it's 'SOS Peck.' That's how a leader addresses a valued member of their team."

Nobody had moved.

Lowenstein had held up two hands in mock defeat, but

his eyes had been hard. "OK, OK. Your point is taken, Walker. Peck, anything to add?"

Lea had given him a huge smile and spoken in a deep, Southern drawl. "Sir, no, sir. Special Agent Walker covered it exceptionally."

Dom had sat.

Now, as she looked over the golf course, Dom calmed her breathing.

Down the line, Lowenstein barked, "Walker."

"I'm in Vegas."

"I heard. I heard through the grapevine. Not even from Fontaine."

She waited him out.

He growled. "This going to be our new normal, Walker?"

"What's that, sir?"

"You running to Fontaine every time you get a new idea?"

She clamped her lips shut.

"One day, I won't be your line manager. It will be a good day."

A long silence built between them.

He finally broke. "What's falling off while you're out there?"

He knew. He knew she was in between live cases and revisiting cold cases. But he wanted to force her to answer to him, a subordinate to a leader. "Only the cold cases."

"Why is it, exactly, that you're calling me?"

"I think there may be something else I need to chase while I'm out here."

He cursed loudly away from the phone, then said, "Inform me. Go ahead, inform me what you're going to do because I know damn well you're not asking for my approval."

"There may be a connection with another cold case we're working."

"Which one?"

"James Pascale."

"The one connected to your lost duckling?"

"Yes, that one."

"What's the new lead?"

"It's remote. I just want to chase it down."

"I'm waiting."

"It's gonna take me to Jackson, Wyoming."

"Did you just say *Wyoming*?"

"Yes." She pushed through the dense silence. "I'll take my weekend up in Jackson. It won't be on Bureau time. I thought you should know."

"Like I said, you're informing me. Not seeking approval."

Yes. That is exactly what I'm doing. But she stayed silent.

He hung up.

In the next moment, she called the number Lea had given her for the cybersecurity firm.

A woman with a soft, velvety voice answered on the second ring. "Vanilla Orchard."

"Brad Johnson, please."

"Whom may I say is calling?"

"Special Agent Domini Walker, FBI." It was always a showstopper.

The woman took a small breath, then said, "Just a moment."

Five minutes later, a male picked up the line. "This is Brad."

"Hi, Brad. Sorry to interrupt."

"It's fine."

"I've got a few questions I'd like to ask about a case I'm looking into."

"That's fine. Go ahead."

The water sprinklers clicked on and thin arcs of spray spiked over the immaculate green. "I'm actually here, at Summit Club. I can come to you."

Chapter Twenty-One

Brad Johnson's house was a modern two-story on a lot of green grass. It was all clean lines and tall windows. Dom pulled into the driveway and parked in front of one of the two garage doors. Outside the car, the heat was dry and stifling.

The unusually wide front door cantilevered open and the white, blond male from the CCTV stepped out. He was a nice-looking guy. Dirty-blond hair, a goatee, light-brown eyes. His shoulders were small, narrow, and his hands looked soft. He had the tepid skin tone of someone who stayed inside a lot, looking at computer screens. "Agent, welcome."

Inside, the expansive living room was immaculate. Gray couches sat on gray, stone floors. Tall stone walls of gray, polished cement reached up through an atrium. A huge white and gray marble island sat under three pendant lamps. The back wall was all windows out onto the immediate green of one section of the golf course. Beyond were the brown rolling hills and mountains.

The murmur of a woman on a business call emerged from a back room.

Brad walked through the kitchen. "Can I get you something to drink?"

There were four used coffee mugs around the sink. "Just some water, thanks."

Opening a double door fridge, he poured a glass of a water from a jug with floating cucumbers. Handing it to her, he nodded to the outdoor patio. "It's still early enough to sit outside."

"Sure."

Once seated, he leaned back and placed crossed fingers on his chest. He exuded an air of calm and curious. "How can I help you, Agent?"

She didn't expect a cybersecurity expert and hacker who had done some prison time at an early age to be an easy interview. He would be resistant. She needed a soft approach. "What type of work does Vanilla Orchard do?"

"We're a cybersecurity firm. We work with clients to secure their networks from intrusion. Mostly."

No hand movements to indicate anxiety. No facial tics. In fact, his face was placid and she wondered if he was on the spectrum. Most people were slightly nervous with a stranger in their home, let alone a law enforcement officer. She said, "This is not my area of expertise. Can you break that down for me, like I don't know much, because I don't really."

"Sure. The most likely intrusions come in a variety of types, Denial of Service (DoS) or Distributed Denial of Service (DDoS) attacks, Man-in-the-Middle (MitM), Phishing or Spear Phishing, Drive-by, and Password Attacks. There are SQL injections, Cross-site Scripting (XSS) , Eavesdropping, and malware."

He was trying to overwhelm her with technical vocabulary. It wasn't going to work. "Can you break some of those down for me?"

"Sure, I can touch on a few. Denial of Service basically overwhelms and disrupts a system so it can't deliver on client requests. Some bad actor just wants to stuff up your delivery of your product via your website. There's no access to your server by the attacker."

"OK."

"Man-in-the-Middle attacks are more intermediary. The attacker gets between the network and the client. The attacker lets the client believe they are communicating with the company server. So, Man-in-the-Middle."

His eyes were steady on her face. Still no outward display of anxiety. "Huh. Interesting."

"Phishing is usually a combo of intrusion and human tricks. The attacker wants to gain personal information to be used in the company server. Very targeted. Often an email spoof. Hard to stop because of the human error element. You know, company staff make mistakes. Open emails."

Sure.

"And then there's malware. That's the worst level of hack, you could say. You want me to keep going?"

Let him think he is still in charge. "This is interesting. Yes, please."

"So, malware is script that is actually inserted onto the server. It will then propagate. This can happen in a number of ways. File infectors. Boot record infectors. Polymorphic viruses. Worms. Self-contained. And ransomware."

"Hmm. Yes, I've heard of malware. What are you working on these days?"

"We're dealing with a Cross-site Script attack. A hacker

has run scripts on a client website. They've figured out how to send the company's clients' cookies to the hacker's server for extraction."

Let's shake this up a bit. "And what type of coding did you produce when you were a hacker?" She knew the answer to this. She'd asked Lea to talk to the cyber team down in Quantico. Brad Johnson had originally been picked up ten years ago for a Trojan that had set up a back door at a bank, which he'd exploited to steal money. More recently, the markers they'd identified that had been used by Ice Pick were something called an Eavesdropping attack. The program allowed Ice Pick to intercept network traffic and get confidential information that he then used to contact the victim.

Brad's hands dropped to his lap in a forced calm. He smiled, but it was fake. "I'm still a hacker. I'm just working on the right side of the law."

"I meant, what type of coding, of the examples you just explained, did you produce when you were on the wrong side of the law?"

He resisted but eventually replied, "I built malware."

Here we go. It's all about the next few minutes. She gazed over the view. "Brad, you didn't ask what I specialize in. But I get it. It's unnerving to be approached by an FBI special agent, let alone to be interviewed." She turned back to him. "That's OK. A lot of people don't know that most FBI special agents specialize." She clasped her fingers and let the palms of her hands rub together, as if preparing for a fight. "I specialize in missing children."

He paled.

"And there's an unusual thing about the landscape that is missing children. The predators are often linked somehow. Sometimes even networked." She stared into his eyes. "Which means, for someone like me, nailing one fucker to the wall often leads us to the next one."

He swallowed.

"That's why agents like me hunt. That's why we take every single lead we've got and we chase it to the ground. We turn over rocks and dive into snake pits. We get down into those viper nests. Vipers don't scare me. Because you just never know which sick child predator is gonna help us identify another one."

His face was pale and slack.

"You see, one in particular has recently used a Trojan horse against a bank. A simple Trojan horse, as it was explained to me. Nothing so elaborate as what you may have produced in the past."

He waited. His eyes were now wide.

"We've attributed it back to you."

He blinked slowly.

"This particular Trojan horse of yours was used to obtain information from a woman named Maria Esposito. That information was then used to break into Maria's ten-year-old son's phone. The son's name is Stevie. A text was sent to Stevie. It looked like it had come from his mother. It told him to meet her at a McDonald's near their home. He went there. We have that on security tape. Then he was taken. Never seen again."

His mouth gaped open slightly.

"I am requesting your help identifying your client who purchased that Trojan horse from you, Mr. Johnson, which was used to kidnap Stevie Esposito."

He licked his lips to break the dryness of his mouth. "I used a broker."

There. Just like that, he'd admitted to the crime — the selling of code for purposes of criminal acts. She waited.

"I use a broker for anything off-grid."

"For anything illegal."

"Yes."

"How often do you do that?"

"Depends. If I need the cash."

She swept her eyes around the patio and out to the golf course. "You don't look like a man who needs cash." Her eyes returned to his face.

"Looks can be deceiving."

"And this broker, what do you call him?"

"'Swiss.' Or 'Suisse.' Either. He uses both."

"Clever. A neutral broker. Just like the neutral country."

"Yes."

"Where did you meet this Swiss?"

"A few years back at Def Con."

"How do I get in touch with this broker of yours?"

He shook his head. "I only have a number. If you think he'll talk to you, he won't. He'll sniff you out in a hot second. Especially if you don't give him a heads-up."

"I'd like to think I'm clever enough to create the proper incentives for Swiss to chat with me. I'll need that number, Brad."

Brad Johnson stood.

She raised a hand. "Give me your personal number too. In case I have some follow-up questions."

He scowled but moved past her to the glass sliding door and went inside.

Out in the driveway, the sun was getting brighter. It felt ten degrees warmer than it had when she'd first arrived. In her right hand was a small piece of paper with two numbers. The first identified as "*Swiss.*" The second was noted *"Brad J."* She snapped a picture of the numbers and filed the picture in a gallery called "Ice Pick."

Chapter Twenty-Two

Owen called Jaimie Spencer in tech to relay the news from Mila: They were looking in an area of Wyoming called the Wind River Basin.

Jaimie had responded, "That's a lot better. I'm almost done with the code. I'll run the search soon."

Owen's second line of forensic attack, christened "Humans Gonna Human" or when he was in a crabby mood, "Humans Can Be Suckers," was a far less methodical approach than Zero In. It involved opportunistically chasing official documents filed with the government to a living, breathing human. The records could include wages, income tax, mortgages, or financial debt. He would build out a spiderweb structure with Maxfield Clafoutis's Lower East Side apartment as the kickoff point with the goal to narrow the search to individuals who may have been related, even tangentially, to the crime. Then he'd sucker the human into revealing important details.

He made himself a coffee and sat down at the dining table.

To determine the owner of a particular apartment in New York took a few relatively simple steps. First, he pulled up the Geographic Online Address Translator, the website portal of the New York's Department of City Planning's Information Technology Division, and entered the street address. It returned a six-digit tax block and lot, or parcel identifier. He plugged that number into the ACRIS website of the New York City's Department of Finance, Office of the City Register's online portal. It fed him the records related to ownership going back to 1987. These records included detailed deeds, mortgage, and mortgage-related banking documents. Variations of the lot and block identifier system was used across the United States in cities and densely populated suburbs.

Scanning the results, he narrowed in on the years Clafoutis could have purchased the listing. The fifth returned document was titled, *12/12/2010 through 06/08/2020, Document type: Deed, Party: Errvan Holding.*

Errvan Holding. Interesting. Like most rich people, Clafoutis's property had been owned by a holding company.

But Owen needed an individual. A human to sucker.

His fingers fanned out over the keyboard.

Twenty minutes later, he sat back in his chair and stared at the screen. He had not been able to identify any individual related to Errvan Holding because it was itself held by a trust named NorthEasterly. He was looking at the well-designed structure of a shell company inside a trust. A lockbox within a safe.

Clafoutis had gone to great lengths to keep his private life hidden. Owen rubbed his palms and clapped. Clafoutis's representative had gone to great lengths to remain anonymous. *I'm coming for you, my sucka.*

Two hours later, he sat back again. He had uncovered the entity that had set up NorthEasterly trust. It was a registered agent named Blue Sky. Its mailing address and telephone were #321 Route 25, Laramie, Wyoming. Tel: 555 232 4590.

Wyoming.

Owen grinned. Both campaigns were homing in on Wyoming. Enough document searching. It was time to reach out and tickle a sucker.

Chapter Twenty-Three

The subway was crowded after lunch. Holding a pole, Mila swayed with the motion of the train on the track. She felt light and optimistic. The shrub discovery that morning had narrowed the investigation to a certain part of Western Wyoming. It was great information for Dom. While it was incremental, it was a step forward. Always moving forward. That was a cause for celebration.

Additionally, the class she'd just sat through of Professor Chow's had been exceptional. She had taken a ton of notes and was excited about the assigned reading, the files on a criminal case from the Eastern District of New York.

Of course she'd continue to pull the threads on any new Jimmy leads, but for now, she was satisfied. Today had been a good day. No, today had been a great day. A ten out of ten.

The wheels of the train clicked against the railway tracks. Click. Click.

The car pulled into the next station and came to a stop.

The doors swooshed open. Passengers jostled out and a new set pushed in.

The doors closed. The train pulled from the station and into the dark tunnel.

Somewhere in the car, something was tapping. Tap. Tap. An older woman with dark glasses was using a white guide cane to make her way down the center aisle. Tap, tap. She felt the back of a seat and settled down.

Mila's mind paused. The woman wasn't constrained by her lack of one of five senses. She relied on others. The thought tickled.

She blinked as her eyes bounced around the car. The blind woman. A young mother with an empty baby stroller. A couple at the far end of the car. These were all sights. One sense. This morning's discovery had been based on photos. The use of only one sense: sight.

What if she used other senses to find clues? She closed her eyes.

Clack, clack. The wheels against the rails underneath the car sped up as the train hit a straightaway.

Woosh. The sound of wind whipping through a crack in a window.

She squeezed her eyes tighter.

Ringing. It was an alarm somewhere in a car out in front.

The whine from the wind pitched slightly higher.

She took the steps two at a time and emerged on Christopher Street. She scrolled through the contacts on her phone and pressed *Archer Robinson*.

He answered on the first ring tone. "Archer."

"Archer, it's Mila Pascale."

"Hi, Mila. How're you doing?"

"OK."

"It's a new day, right?"

"Yes, it is. Can I ask you a question?"

"Of course."

"On the missing persons posters, they have the local law enforcement number and NCMEC's number."

"Yes."

"And those calls are recorded."

"Yes. NCMEC keeps all those."

"So the person with the tip, they would call one or the other."

"Correct." He paused. "What are you thinking, Mila?"

"What if Jimmy was transported?"

"It's a legitimate question."

"What if he ended up out west, like Wyoming or Montana something?"

"OK? What are you thinking?"

"Let's say someone saw something suspicious. Maybe an older man with a boy who looked troubled."

"Yes?"

"But that eyewitness saw the boy in Wyoming. They would naturally call either the local police or NCMEC."

"OK?"

"In that case, they wouldn't know it matched the photo of James Pascale because Jimmy's posters are assigned to and shown in New York."

"OK?"

She took a deep breath. "I need to listen to all the recorded calls that have come in to NCMEC and all local police since Jimmy went missing in 2015."

Archer blew out an exhale. "Mila—"

"How many calls do you think that is?"

"Nationwide? To both NCMEC and local police?"

"Yes."

He whistled. "I don't know."

"But NCMEC has a database of all those calls?"

"I mean, anything that was identified as a call pertaining to a missing person, yes."

"Going back to 2015?"

"Yes."

"Can you send me a copy of that database?"

"Mila, that would take days, weeks — months, maybe." He relented. "You sure you want to do this?"

"Yes."

He sighed. "OK. I'll send it when I get it."

"Thanks, Archer."

Before he hung up, he warned, "Mila, it's gotta be thousands of calls. Manage your expectations."

In fact, there were 9,356 calls made to local law enforcement or NCMEC since 2015 and they arrived three hours later via a zipped file attached to an email from Archer with the cover note, *"Please take your time."*

With a new slice of pizza, she opened the file. Folders were organized by state and year. Four hundred and fifty folders. A single folder was titled "*UNNAMED.*" She opened it. There were over a hundred audio files that were simply numbered. Over the years, these audio files had been misnamed. Human error.

She retreated to the main index and opened the folder titled *WYOMING 2015*. Inside, each audio file was labeled with the state initials and date.

She slipped on headphones and her skin turned clammy. This was going to be hideous.

She clicked open the first, *WY_ 01_02_2015* and hit *play*.

The recording was an older woman with a weak voice. "I am calling about a photo of a missing person. I think I saw that girl at the gas station on Hendrix and Plymouth on Sunday. Maybe you can go there and look at their security camera. Good luck."

Somehow, she would have to set up a logical process to go through over nine thousand audio files. Priority. Efficiency.

She would set up her own folder and copy in every recording. Then she would tag them as *No*, *Maybe*, and *Yes* in terms of relevancy.

Later she would dig into the *Yes* files first.

If nothing turned up, she would dig into the *Maybe* recordings.

Priority. Efficiency.

This first recording was about a girl. This would not be a lead. She labeled it *No* and moved to the next one.

On the tenth recording she hit a *Maybe*. A woman's voice said, "My name is Rebecca Hasselhoff. I'm calling...I believe I might have a tip. I saw a notice on my Facebook feed. A young boy. I think I may have seen him at the Kentucky Fried Chicken over by the Midas on Lincoln Highway in Cheyenne last week. Please feel free to call me if you want any further details." She rattled off a number.

Mila jotted down the number, closed the file, and tagged it as *Maybe*. She would revisit it during the next pass.

Keep moving. Priority. Efficiency.

Chapter Twenty-Four

The Jackson Hole airport terminal was a cavernous space with wide wood beams across a slatted wood ceiling, black-and-white posters of mountains and hills, and expansive windows with a view of a sunset across a snowcapped mountain range. In the center of the space, a huge, bronze statue of an antlered elk bellowed at the skylight, as if angry at the blue sky beyond.

Ten minutes later, Dom circled out of the airport in a rented Dodge Journey, past a second statue of a cowboy on a bouncing horse. The cowboy's left hand, thrown up behind him, whipped a Stetson in the air.

She flipped up the collar on her coat against the chill in the car. *I am a long way from New York.*

Earlier, Lea had sent her directions to the location of the Wort Hotel, Jackson Hole. Her note had read, "Take a moment, warrior sister." She had included a detour a short distance from downtown Jackson Hole.

Darkness descended as she sped south along Route 191 and the Dodge's headlights beamed across the empty two-lane highway. As she entered the north side of Jackson Hole, a full moon appeared in the east. Lights beamed from squared tops and gabled roofs of the iconic false storefronts. Clapboard siding and blinking marquee letters on billboards harkened back to the Old West of gold rushes and unclaimed land.

She followed the directions through town and took a left heading east on East Broadway, passing a log cabin motel, a smattering of clean houses, and a medical center. She could make out a small bluff on the horizon. Passing the last house, the Dodge was doused in blue moonlight. Up ahead, a big wooden sign read, *National Elk Refuge*.

She slowed and rumbled over a grate onto the smaller Elk Refuge Road edged by tall pine trees. *Lea, how come you're so smart?*

When the road opened up to a vast field, she pulled over, parked, and rolled down the windows. The chilly night air blew through the prairie grass and swept through the interior of the car. The moon was bright in the sky.

She extinguished the motor and rested her head against the headrest. Domini Walker was no longer in the city.

At first, she listened to the sound of nature. The wind, the birds, the rustling. But soon she was listening to her own breathing and her mind began to wander. Lately, it had felt like her life was shifting. The tightness around her was loosening.

For most of her adult life, it had been Dom and Beecher. Beecher and Dom. Two fighters in a harsh world. When he had moved away to college, she had checked in on him regularly and he had spent many weekends at home with her. When he had married too early, she had been there to witness the young mistakes and had hugged him when he'd moved back after the divorce.

Ever since Mila had moved in, life felt somehow more stable. It was as if, instead of being horribly disruptive, the young woman's quirks had muted the intensity of life's hardships, expanding the small, protected world she and Beecher had crafted.

In the car, she smiled to herself. Mila was a character. Blunt, odd, widely optimistic. She could be funny and serious in the same second. She spun puns and jokes and cracked up when an actor in a movie vomited. She liked order, timeliness, and set patterns. She went into her room every night to study and didn't emerge until the next morning. She loved dogs.

Dom frowned. The hunt for Jimmy Pascale was treacherous. It was likely they wouldn't find anything but a dead end. She'd seen that so many times. But if they did find him, it could be horrendous. Bad things happened to kidnapped kids. Dom wanted to wrap her arms around Mila and protect her, the way she had Beecher. But she knew the young woman had her own journey.

When Mila graduated and got into Quantico, she would still be part of their lives. She had become an integral member of the family. Just like that. So quick. So easy.

Dom wondered if this was how it always was with someone who was destined to be in your life in a meaningful way.

Owen's smile crossed her mind.

She turned the key in the ignition and the motor revved. It was time to quit all this daydreaming and get some sleep.

Chapter Twenty-Five

Outside, over Elizabeth Street Park, the moon was high and bright against the dark sky. The sounds of the bustling city — cars cruising down the streets, the sound of a truck's heavy brakes, the clang of a steel door — were soothing against Mila's jangled nerves.

She had made it through all of Wyoming's audio files as well as those in the surrounding states of Montana, South Dakota, Nebraska, Colorado, Utah, and Idaho. That meant she had cleared fifty-six folders and listened to over five hundred recordings. Most of those she had tagged as *No*. They were either tips about women or children who did not match Jimmy's age at the time of the call. Twenty-three were tagged as *Maybe*. None were tagged as a *Yes*.

She stood and stretched. At this rate, she would make it another five hours before she had to go to class. She had the ability to not sleep if required. And this required. She was on a hunt, and she was bearing down.

She munched on a pizza slice to keep her strength and made a third pot of coffee.

Settling into the armchair, she slipped on the headphones and opened up the *UNNAMED* folder. One hundred twenty-two recordings. It didn't matter what order she listened to them; she just needed to properly tag them.

She randomly chose one and hit *play*.

The line was open. There was only background noise, as if in nature.

A sniff.

She clamped her fingers to the headphones. *Was that a sniff?*

Sniff.

Yes, a small sniff. The sniff of a small person.

The hair on her arms stood straight. She dropped her head and concentrated on the noise.

More background noise. A louder hum.

She closed her eyes to focus on the sounds.

Through the hum came a muffled boom, like a very distant cymbal crash.

Was that thunder?

Sniff.

She squeezed her eyes tighter.

A small voice whispered, "Lala."

A frozen blade sliced down her spine as the air in her lungs punched outward. Her head jerked up.

There was only the background hum.

She squeezed the earphones tighter.

The tiny voice said again, "Lala?"

Her lungs were iced. She mouthed, "Jimmy?"

A male voice from a distance said, "Cone."

A man. It had been a man. *No, he hadn't said cone; he'd said, "Come."*

The man said more words, but they were indecipherable.

She swallowed against a parched throat.

There was a loud clang.

She startled and her eyes flew open.

Jimmy had dropped the phone. But the hum continued because the phone was dangling on its cord.

Pick up the phone, Jimmy. I'm here!

The hum continued and, in the distance, more thumping.

Jimmy! I'm here! Pick it back up!

Crunch. Crunch. Footfalls on gravel.

Was Jimmy returning? Not a single cell in her body moved.

Click. The line went dead.

She yanked off the headphones, scrambled for the mouse, and pulled up the file name. It was a disordered mess. *CKE_JK_2015_F_WY.* There was no associated phone number. Her brain pounded.

WY stands for Wyoming.

2015 is the year of the call. It was the same year Jimmy had been stolen.

F is February.

The conclusion swept over her. The month after he had been taken, Jimmy had called for her help. No one had known what to do with the call and someone at NCMEC had given the audio file a terrible, illogical name.

Jimmy.

His voice from the darkness. Lost. Forgotten.

Jimmy.

There had been a man with him. Telling him what to do.

Mila jerked to the right as the half-digested pizza exploded up her throat and out of her mouth.

Part IV

Chapter Twenty-Six

Monnie Friday didn't have a lot to go on when it came to Dakota's case. The big man had a house near Pinedale that overlooked a dark lake, had hunting trophies on the wall, and also housed a large statue of a cowboy on a horse. That described ninety percent of the big homes owned around Pinedale.

She scratched fingernails across her scalp and glanced around the spartan, spotless room of the Sheriff's Department. The sheriff was, per usual, out at the film location. One of the four Riverton officers, who she nicknamed "Fisheye," was out at a meeting with a rancher about a missing cow. Singular. One missing cow. The police had been called out for a missing cow. The other two officers, whom she'd nicknamed "Nosebleed" and "Eyesore," were silently, mindlessly playing solitaire on their computers.

No one was looking for Anton Norris. A headache pounded both temples and she rubbed dry eyes.

Two weeks earlier, Sheriff Kantore had called off the searches. He had sent home the volunteers. A week ago, he'd convened the last press briefing on the top of the building's front stairs. His voice had been resolute. "We are actively continuing our search for Anton. We call on everyone in the community to keep an eye out for anything out of the ordinary."

But Monnie knew that were not *actively* doing anything. They hadn't turned up any new evidence or leads since the day Anton had gone missing.

Except Dakota had given her some clues.

Big Man had gone into the Mountain View Diner, identified that Dakota was on his own, and deceived the boy into getting into his truck. Very intentional. Had Big Man been sitting in the diner the whole time? Had he observed Dakota coming in alone and being aided by the waitress? Had he made a plan to kidnap the boy in that moment? Or was always he on the lookout for lonely, easily-picked-off boys?

The Mountain View Diner was a clean place on Route 789 as you made your way north into Riverton. It was open twenty-four hours. She'd spoken to the waitress, Evelyn, the day before and had typed up the notes.

Eyewitness remembered the victim. "Oh, yeah. He looked hungry. And dirty. I gave him a meal, found his mom's number, called her and then called you all. Next thing I knew, he was gone. I just assumed you'd all come and gotten him."

Establishment does not have security camera.

Not a lot of businesses did in Riverton. Small petty theft was the most likely crime. Not enough returns to invest in high-tech security stuff.

Monnie sat back and reviewed the short report before hitting the *print* button. Rising from her desk, she walked the single sheet of paper into the sheriff's office and set it on his tidy desk.

She could almost hear him now. He'd step through his doorframe and waffle the paper. "Friday. There's nothing to this. This all you got from the diner?"

Nosebleed and Eyesore would glance up from their desks.

She'd reply, "Yes."

"We still got nothing."

She'd respond, "You're right."

The sheriff didn't believe there was a connection between Dakota and Anton. In fact, the sheriff didn't believe the Big Man story at all. He didn't believe in the potential for a serial kidnapper in their midst. He'd turn and drop the paper in the 'to file' box on his shelf.

Nosebleed and Eyesore would return to their interminable games.

The investigation into a big man hunting young boys from the Wind River Reservation would officially stay open. But here, inside the sheriff's office, it was a done deal. Closed. Unresolved.

But for Monnie Friday, the investigation was ongoing because she had omitted from the report something Evelyn had told her. Around the same time that Dakota had been eating his turkey meal around the corner of the counter, a large group had entered the diner.

"Nobody I recognized," is what Evelyn had said.

"How many?"

"Maybe ten?"

It was unusual.

Most folks in this part of the country dined alone or in small, family groups. Especially folks from out of town. Tourists, travelers.

Monnie had asked, "Men and women?"

"Yeah. Both."

"Did you happen to notice their vehicles?"

"Nah. Too busy."

"But they came and sat all together?"

"Took up three booths, all back-to-back."

"And left together?"

"Oh yeah, ordered, ate, left together."

"Loud?"

"Nah. They were sober."

"Did you get the sense they were on the clock, maybe? Working together?"

"Yeah, maybe."

Monnie hadn't put that nugget of information into the report. Because she didn't want the sheriff to directly tell her not to pursue it.

The only folks who traveled in packs of ten around Riverton were the film crews.

And everybody knew it.

Chapter Twenty-Seven

Her phone vibrated and Dom opened her eyes. It took a moment to place the slatted, wooden ceiling, but then she remembered it was the Wort Hotel in Jackson Hole, Wyoming. Downstairs, the famous old hotel had a grand entrance with an imposing central staircase, a huge, stone fireplace surrounded by high wingback chairs, and walls busy with oil paintings of buffalo, cowboys, and prairie.

She rolled over the bed, sunk into thick feathers and picked up her phone. There was a text from Owen. *"You up for a call?"*

Despite her earlier resentment, she felt an uptick in her heartbeat.

She pushed the call button and his phone rang. His deep voice was scratchy. "Morning."

She closed her eyes and savored the sound. "Hi."

"How's Jackson?"

"It's pretty lovely, actually."

"How's the Wort Hotel?"

She opened her eyes and grinned. "It's pretty lovely."

"You get in late?"

"Timing was good." She told him about her drive out to into the dark wilderness.

"Yeah, that does sound nice. You ever think about leaving the city?"

She knew he was a big outdoor sports person and wondered what he thought. She hedged. "I haven't, but I guess I'm keeping an open mind."

"Yeah, same. Like I'm not adverse to it, but I love the city."

Relief swept through her. *What was happening?*

He said, "And life changes, priorities change."

Her heart fluttered. Wary solo travelers. "Exactly." *Time to change the subject.* She took a deep breath. "Fontaine told me you've asked to be reassigned."

"Listen, about that. I owe you an apology. A big one. I was going to tell you before anyone else. In person. But it came up unexpectedly in a meeting with my boss. He asked directly and I couldn't weave around it. Dom, I'm sorry you didn't hear it from me."

The resentment started to lift. "OK."

"I know that you wanted me involved so that I could keep an eye on the case. We both want to nail him. It's just… Well, I felt like…" He took a long moment. "It would have meant putting up a very real wall between us. I wasn't ready to do that."

It was a big confession. He'd chosen her over the case of a career. The resentment evaporated.

He chuckled softly. "Wow, this conversation turned heavy fast."

She smiled. His timing was exceptional. "A bit."

"Right?" He exhaled. "But trust me, I'm not rushing this. I just… I don't know, I wanted this to have a chance."

The sunrise pinkened the window. *Me too.* "I get it."

He blew through his lips. "You know how I'm going to that therapist to get the all-clear from the shooting?"

"Yes."

"And that my mother is a psychologist?"

"Yes."

"Well, they are both kinda telling me that I need to go vulnerable." Long pause. "That part of giving something a chance, is…is that…I have to learn how to be vulnerable."

Adrenaline shot through her system. She could barely breathe.

His voice was soft. "Sorry, I know that's super heavy."

She found her voice. "It's OK. I get it. I do. It's funny. Lea, of all people, is telling me something very similar."

"Oh, good, then my $50 worked?"

She laughed out loud. "Traitor."

He laughed. "OK, so listen, let's kinda just pretend it's not that heavy, you know? Like, I made a decision to just get off an investigation, it happens to be one that involves your dad, and it's just better all-around that I'm not it. No need to, you know, pull that into whatever is happening between you and me."

God, he was so healthy. *Maybe I could learn something from him?* She scratched her ear. "That seems like a really good idea."

"Oh, good. OK. Let's move on."

"Agreed."

"I've talked to both Lea and Mila. I mean, it's the crew, right?" He chuckled. "Anyway, since I have the weekend before I'm back to Javitz, I did some sniffing."

She sat up against the headboard. "You don't have to do that."

"It's Mila we're talking about. Of course I do."

Warmth spread across her chest.

"I mean, that's why you're out there, am I right?"

"You're a good man, Owen."

"Whoa, whoa, we agreed no more heavy today."

She chuckled. "Just giving you a compliment."

"Warning. Danger! Heavy!"

She laughed. "OK, OK. You're a terrible person."

"That's better. What's your day look like?"

They sounded like a couple. "I'm chatting with the Bureau guy here."

"Nice."

"You?"

"I think I might make some calls."

"Thank you."

"No need to thank me."

She could stay on the phone with him for hours.

As if reading her mind, he said, "Listen, before we hang up, I did hear something about the Velk case. Since I'm not on it, I can relay it to you."

Her heart clenched. "I'm all ears."

"Gessen and the others are claiming Velk gave them immunity."

The air pushed from her chest. "In exchange for what?"

"That is exactly the question, Dom. Rumor has it he promised not to ever prosecute them for misconduct if they protected his life."

"From the Brighton mob."

"That's my guess too."

"Oh, shit."

"Yeah, it's a huge fact."

"And evidence of guilt."

"Absolutely."

"And RICO."

"Absolutely."
"And it's another nail in his trial coffin."
"Let's hope."
"Thank you, Owen."
"No need to thank me. We're in this together."
Her heart swelled.

Chapter Twenty-Eight

Exactly five buildings south of the New Museum on Bowery, a hot-pink door stood out among gray storefronts. A brass plaque across the top of the door read, *Zills Production*. Mila pulled it open and stepped inside. Bright spotlights picked up various paintings and photos on three black walls. A young Black man with smooth skin and dreadlocks looked up from behind a sleek, glass table. He asked quizzically, "Can I help you?"

Keep it calm. Sound normal. "Yes. I need help."

He eyed her warily. "Uh, OK?"

Do not sound different. "I need help getting better clarity on a recording."

It took him a second to understand. "Oh, no, we don't do that here. We're a recording studio. For musicians—"

"Yes, I understand this. I need someone to help me." Her face had contorted. She took a deep breath to calm her voice. "I have a problem. I need some help."

He insisted. "Look, kid, you came to the wrong place. We don't just take walk-ins. Like a hair salon—"

Mila felt shaky. "But it won't take long. Maybe I could just talk to someone who works the technical—"

He was getting agitated. "Kid, I'm telling you, we don't do that."

From behind her, the pink door opened and a tall, broad-shouldered woman with long, red hair stepped in. "Hey, Rav," she said to the Black guy. She gave Mila a smile as she strode past.

Rav nodded to Mila. "She was just leaving."

Mila's voice cracked and tears of frustration stung the back of her eyes. "I need help."

The woman paused and turned back. "What's that?" She had a British accent.

Rav insisted, "She's got the wrong place, Fi. It's OK."

Mila stepped toward Fi. "I need help. It won't take long. I just need help with a recording. To make it clearer." She blinked back tears.

Rav sighed. "I keep telling her we don't do that here."

Fi cocked her head and spoke slowly to Mila. "You have a recording?"

Mila nodded. "I do. It could be…important."

Rav sat back and crossed his arms.

Give context. Mila took a deep breath. "My brother went missing. Seven years ago. I am working with the National Center for Missing and Exploited Children. They have sent me recordings of calls to their tip line. Thousands of them. I think I have found an old recording of my brother."

Fi's mouth dropped open and she whispered, "Jesus."

Mila held out a thumb drive. "The recording has noises I can't hear clearly. I just need help. To make them clearer."

Fi blinked. "That may be the most tragic thing I've heard in a long time."

Mila swallowed.

Fi waved her toward the back door. "You come on back here, little thing, and we'll work some magic."

Rav shook his head in disbelief.

The work room was long and thin, painted in deep gray. At the far end sat a large console with buttons, sliders, and lights. Above it was four huge screens. On either side stood tall speakers.

Fi dropped her bag on one of the two plush, red armchairs by the door and clicked on dim overhead lights. "Welcome to my lair. My name is Fiona Grandini, Fi, and I'm the chief mastering engineer here at Zills. This is where the magic happens." She pulled up a rolling chair beside hers and sat at the console. "Here, sit next to me. What's your name?"

"Mila," she said as she sat. "Pascale."

Fi held out her hand. "Well, Mila, let's hear what you've got."

Mila cleared her throat and held out the thumb drive.

Fi took it gingerly and slid it into a desktop. "This is a recording we think of your brother to a tip line." She glanced sideways at Mila. "He's been missing."

Mila said softly, "Yes."

Fi opened the file on her screen and spoke with authority. "Right. This is what we're going to do. We're going to listen to the original and then we'll see what we can do to help clean up anything that's not clear." Her finger hovered over the mouse and she eyed Mila. "You OK?"

Mila nodded. "It's the first break in the case since he's been gone."

Fi nodded. Her eyes were gentle. "Here we go."

Mila dropped her chin to her chest and closed her eyes.

The phone call audio boomed across the speakers.

The two sniffs.

The small voice that said "Lala" twice.

The male voice, "Come."

The background noise of the hum, the buzz, the squeal, the boom, and the clang.

The footfalls approaching the phone.

The silences of a dead line.

Fi asked softly, "You think that's your missing brother?"

Mila opened her eyes and lifted her head. "That was his nickname for me. Lala."

Fi blinked back tears. "You OK to keep going?"

She swallowed against the raw, sour taste of fear in her throat. "I must."

"Yes, we must." Fi turned back to the screen, her fingers moving like second nature across the console. "I'm going to pull up a spectrogram. It will help us visualize what's going on here. I'm pretty sure that hum is the phone line, and the other background noises sound organic — but we'll get to the bottom of it."

On the screen, a colorful series of complicated waveforms with valleys and peaks appeared against a black background. The waves were superimposed over vertical and horizontal axes.

Fi said, "This program visualizes the track. Those peaks in blue are the most prominent sounds. Those are the voices. We can already hear them enough. We know what they say. I'll clean them out. That OK with you?"

Mila nodded. *It is very OK to not have to hear young Jimmy or the kidnapper again.*

Three peaks disappeared.

She nodded to the screen. "Let's figure out that lowest wave."

A low drone emanated from the speakers.

She slowed the audio and hit *play* again.

A consistent, slower purr.

Fi said, "Yup. That's a high frequency buzz. I'm pretty sure it has to do with the phone line. I'm going to clean that out."

The lowest wave disappeared.

"I'm going to focus on those background noises. I'll start with that pattern that is repeated six times across the recording." Fi isolated the first concentrated group of scattered dots and hit *play*.

A warble.

Fi leaned in toward the speaker, clanking on the keyboard, and played a slower rendition of the sound.

A loud gurgle.

Fi nodded to herself. "Yes. That's gotta be running water. And it repeats itself six times. Yes, this is water running over rocks."

Mila said, "Like a creek or a river."

"Bigger than a creek. Sounds like it may be moving swiftly, like white water or something."

Mila nodded.

Fi removed the six repeating patterns. She pointed to a double peak formation. "I want to know what that is."

A hiss and a squeal exploded through the speakers.

Mila jerked in her chair.

Fi said, "Well, that's a very definitive pair. What is that? Let me slow that down."

A longer hiss. A shorter, higher-pitched squeal.

Mila whispered, "Air brakes. Like on a train."

Fi glanced at her.

Mila said, "I hear it in the subways."

"Exactly. That's exactly what it is. That hiss is the air and then the wheel is squealing as it tightens on the rail." Fi's fingers flew. "My bet is that this other pattern here is the wheels turning on the rail."

Clank. Clank. Clank.

Fi nodded emphatically. "Yup. This is definitely a train. You've got a train near a river." She glanced at Mila. "How you holding up?"

"I'm OK."

Fi pointed to a sloping plateau in the middle of the recording. "Let's tease this bugger out. It grows in volume."

A faint murmur grew louder then disappeared.

Mila asked, "Thunder? In the distance?"

"But it drops quickly. Thunder doesn't just end like that." She hit *replay*.

A soft roar gained intensity then dissipated.

Fi said, "It's almost like it's not the original sound... I don't know how to describe that."

Mila whispered, "An echo of something?"

"Maybe? I can't tell."

Again, the muted rumble gained power then vanished.

Mila asked, "Is it muffled?"

"Yes. Muffled. But that doesn't make any sense." Fi tapped her lips together. "I don't even know what to do with this. I'm not sure we're going to decipher this."

Mila's voice was soft. "We must."

Fi glanced at her. "Yes, you're right. We must."

Mila pointed to the screen. "Well, we know it happens before the brakes."

Fi carried on the thought. "So a train brakes, but before it does, it emits this low echo-sounding noise—"

Mila stiffened. "A tunnel. The train is emerging from a tunnel."

Fi whispered. "I'll be damned." Fi sagged into her chair. "Oh my god. Of course."

Mila gathered up her bag. "Thank you, Fi. Thank you."

Fi nodded. "I'm really sorry, Mila. I know that doesn't give you a ton to go on. A river, a train, and a tunnel."

Mila rose. "It's more than you'd think." *How many functioning rail tunnels could there be in the Wind River Basin?*

Chapter Twenty-Nine

Yesterday, the Humans Gonna Human campaign had proven extremely productive. It was time to see where it could lead. From his dining room table, Owen picked up the burner phone and turned it on. There was plenty of battery.

He looked down at his notes and dialed the number in Laramie, Wyoming.

A woman answered, "Blue Sky Agent."

"Hi. Good morning. I'm interested in speaking with someone about purchasing a ranch and I'd like that in a trust."

"Great. Just a moment."

Five minutes later, a second woman picked up. "Janelle Wisker. With whom am I speaking?"

The deception came easily. It was a character he had used many times. In a calm, somewhat timid voice, he answered, "My name is John Zokov. I'm calling from New York."

"Yes, I see that area code. Thanks for calling, Mr. Zokov. What can I do for you?"

He explained in more detail that a friend in New York had worked with Blue Sky and recommended them. He was interested in purchasing property in the Wind River Basin and wanted it to be set up in a trust. He implied he was extremely wealthy and that this may not be the only property he could purchase.

Wisker was smooth. "Absolutely, that's what many of our clients, both domestic and international, do. They use a trust to help protect their assets. Is it only the one property you'd like put within a trust at this time?" Milking him for other business.

"I have other trusts."

"I'm sure you do, Mr. Zokov. Just out of curiosity, what are the residencies of your other trusts? I want to make sure you're getting all the protection and services you could."

"Oh, I have some out of Cayman, of course, and Luxembourg." The ease with which he spoke of the other countries added to the deception.

"Well, as I'm sure you must know, Wyoming acting as an agent has a lot of advantages. As I'm sure your friend has indicated. Should you ever decide to move additional assets, please know I stand ready. We work exclusively with UHNW." She meant ultra-high net worth, a banking term for individuals worth at least $30 million. The number of UHNW individuals in the world fluctuated, given market ups and downs. Generally, they made up six percent of the global population and half of them lived in the US. Wisker was making the distinction that Blue Sky did not work with very high net worth or high net worth, whose assets were in the range of $5 million or $1 million respectively.

"Yes, understood. And in terms of due diligence, Ms.

Wisker, I'll need my family office to conduct ours on both you and your partners."

"Absolutely. We welcome that level of scrutiny by our clients."

"Which accounting firms do you use?"

"For global interests, we use Ernest and Young."

Very credible. He jotted down *EY* on the notebook by his phone. "And for Wyoming properties?"

"We use a very reliable firm that has been around for a hundred years. Breyer Financials. B-R-E-Y-E-R."

He added to *Breyer Financials* to his list. "Is that who will be cutting the checks for utilities, mortgage, what not?"

"That's correct."

"And which lawyers do you use?"

"For global, we use two of the top five firms and for Wyoming, we use Wilcox and James here in Laramie."

He added *Wilcox and James* to the list. "How about real estate agents whom Blue Sky may use?"

"We have a few."

"All based in Laramie?"

"Oh no. We have contacts across the state. In fact, we have someone based in Riverton who covers the Wind River Basin."

"Excellent. Can I get that name too? Just for due diligence purposes."

She spelled the name for Mr. Wellington Horton and a phone number.

Owen concluded. "This sounds quite amenable. I appreciate your help on this, Ms. Wisker."

"We are happy to oblige and are here for you, Mr. Zokov. In terms of our own due diligence, would you mind so much to have your family office call us?"

"Absolutely. I'll tell them." But he wouldn't. Because he

had all the information he needed and Janelle Whisker would never hear from him again.

Chapter Thirty

There were three flights a day via United from New York's JFK through Denver and into Riverton, Wyoming. Before the flight, Mila had looked up Dr. Sebastian Klenck, Professor of Environmental Science and Health at Central Wyoming College. He taught a number of courses, including Geographic Information System Databases. She'd called him from JFK as she'd been boarding and explained that as an NYU criminal justice student, she was researching a cold case in the Wind River Basin and was on her way to meet him.

His response had been appropriately firm for an educator. "Mila, that sounds interesting. But your journey is certainly a bit extreme. We can talk through this over the phone."

If she was even one inch closer to finding Jimmy, she was going to take it.

I am coming to Riverton. One hundred percent. "Professor, it's fine. I got a cheap flight. I land at noon." *Sound normal, Mila!* She didn't need a curious professor to get in her way. "Sir,

I've also never been to Wyoming and I'm quite excited by the trip."

"How old are you, my dear?"

"I'm a senior."

"Do your parents know about this?"

Don't lie. "My parents are not involved in my life, Professor."

"Uh. Yes. OK, well, then. Call me when you get here. I can meet you in my lab." He gave her the campus address.

The small plane landed with a few heavy jumps and a passenger in the back clapped. The captain said, "Welcome to Wyoming, folks."

Mila called Lea, who answered quickly. "Mila, now is not the time."

"But—"

"No, seriously, now is not the time. Oh, and don't bother Dom, either. She's in the middle of stuff. Sorry." She hung up.

Mila pulled down her backpack from the overhead bin, stepped briskly down the airstairs, and followed the line of passengers into the one-terminal Riverton Regional airport.

Sun belted in through the walls of glass. Stuffed birds, a huge moose head, and antlers hung on the walls. It felt very much like one of the exhibit halls in the American Museum of Natural History.

She was the only passenger who headed to the rental car desk.

Thirty minutes later, she was pulling onto the empty US Highway 26 in a compact Chevrolet Spark. She had only ever driven a car a few times in high school driving class, but the concepts were simple. Press the gas to accelerate, brake to slow and stop, and use the turn signals to change lanes. *How hard could it be?*

The GPS instructions were also very simple. It was a six-minute straight line along this road to the college campus.

She pressed down on the pedal and accelerated up to fifty miles per hour along the empty road. Her heart jumped in her chest, but she breathed in deeply.

Straight line to campus. Six minutes.

The landscape of Riverton was a flat prairie surrounded in the far distance by hills. No mountains in sight. Wind River Basin.

A basin.

The clean four-lane road swept through brown scrub and pine copses. Houses and small business buildings dotted both sides. A few cars passed her, but the traffic was almost nothing. This was a long way from New York City.

Ahead, the sign rose for Central Wyoming College and she clicked on the left turn signal in anticipation.

The college drive meandered through wide green lawns with clacking water sprinklers.

The GPS instructed her to turn into a small parking lot behind a main building.

Her hands trembled as she turned off the ignition and she held them in front of her eyes. *This is unusual. But chasing a missing brother is unusual.*

She lifted out her backpack, stood from the car, and locked the door. Crossing through a pedestrian roundabout, she located the professor's building just as he had instructed.

The door to his office on the second floor was open.

She tapped on the frame.

A man in his sixties with bony shoulders looked up from his desk. "Mila Pascale?" he asked with a grin.

She nodded and stepped in.

He stood and held out his hand. He looked kind. "Well, you really came, didn't you?" His nose was flat and his eyes were gray.

"Thanks for seeing me, Professor."

"Sit, sit. Now tell me about this case."

Context. She clasped her hands against the trembles and took a deep breath. She explained the case of a missing boy who had called in to NCMEC and how, with the help of a professional, she had isolated the noises on the recording.

He was impressed. "Oh, what did you all find?"

"The missing boy called from a location, I believe in the Wind River Basin, and that had the following key identifiers: a river, a train track, and a tunnel."

"Extraordinary. This is for a class of yours?"

She nodded. *A small lie. A necessary white lie.*

"And then you tracked me down?"

Finally, the important point. "Yes. I was hoping you could identify for me anywhere in Wind River that has that combination. I've looked up the rail systems out here—"

He held up a hand to pause her. "I won't need a map. Mila, this is going to be easier than you may have expected. I know Wyoming like the back of my hand. Born and raised here. Along with my family. There are six rail companies currently operating in the state: Bighorn Divide and Wyoming Railroad; BNSF Railway Company; Rapid City, Pierre & Eastern Railroad; Swan Ranch Railroad; Union Pacific Railroad; and Wyoming Operation Lifesaver. Of those, only BNSF has a route that includes a tunnel mouth by a river. That would be up in Boysen State Park. The

BNSF rail runs opposite Route 20 on the opposite side of the Bighorn River. There's a tunnel entrance, I'd say, about forty miles up Route 20." He stood, pulled down a huge book, and slapped it on his table. Opening up the dog-eared pages, he flipped through before smoothing down a page and pointing. "Here. That's the tunnel."

She rose, slightly unsteady, and leaned over the table to the map and the location where his finger rested.

Jimmy had been right there. She knew it in her bones. "That's the only rail tunnel by a river?"

"In the Wind River Basin, yes."

She pulled out her phone and took a photo.

He grinned at her. "Going to see for yourself?"

The lump in her throat was too big. All she could do was nod.

His brow crinkled. "What year did you say this crime happened?"

"2015."

"So you're just going to get a feel for the location?"

She nodded again.

He watched her closely and a frown formed. "It's a long way for you to come."

She stiffened. "Yes."

He nodded with understanding.

Tears stung the back of her eyes.

He said, "I hope you find what you're looking for."

She cleared her throat. "Thank you."

"Good luck, Mila Pascale."

Chapter Thirty-One

Jackson Hole's Bureau guy, Roy Cross, was an older gentleman with a bald head, chubby cheeks, and rheumy, brown eyes. He looked near or even past retirement. His handshake was strong. "You're a long way from home, Agent."

"Comes with the job."

"It sure does." He ushered her into the side office. "How's Barry Lowenstein?"

Interesting that you know who my boss is. She cocked her head.

He said nonchalantly, "I always do my homework on visitors." He indicated for her to sit across from his big desk. "He just got promoted, right?"

"Yup."

He shook his head as he sat. "He treating you all OK?"

Interesting. "Why do you ask?"

"'Cause when I knew him on a case a long while ago, he could be an asshole. Maybe they trained it out of him in management school."

"They didn't."

He gave her a half-smile that didn't reach his blue eyes. "Sorry about that."

She shrugged. "You didn't choose."

"That's true." He crossed his leg over the other. "What can I do for you?"

"I've got an odd one. A long cold case."

"Missing kid?"

Again, interesting. She gave him another quizzical look.

"Homework. I noted that's your specialty. I was impressed with the Saint Christopher case. You did an exceptional job."

This was one thorough field agent. The yearlong Saint Christopher case had crisscrossed the country. In the end, they had rescued thirty children being held as sex slaves and shut down a ring. "Well, yes. It's a missing boy, taken at ten years old from New York. Cold case now seven years."

"A cold case."

She nodded.

"I was a bit nervous you were here about a live one."

Careful, Dom, careful. You are about to tread on his backyard. "Well, it's interesting you say that. I've got a family member of the missing boy, who herself is quite a researcher. She's a quirky one, very into numbers and statistics. Also, tenacious. Every year, she digs in more. Historically, she hasn't found anything worth pursuing. But this year, she has brought some finds to my attention." She explained the discovery of the photos of Clafoutis, the Wort Hotel mug, the strikingly familiar-looking boy, and the identifying shrub. "Porter's Sagebrush, I think she called it. From Wind River Basin."

"Wind River. That's Police Chief Kantore's domain. Shaun Kantore. With a K and ending in an E."

"You know him?"

"He and I have a lot in common…"

She waited him out.

"Jackson Hole and Wind River are big with the Hollywood types. The celebs and the wealthy love Jackson Hole as a vacation ground in the winter. The film types love Wind River for their movies. All around that neck of the woods, there are just big landscapes. Hills, mountains, streams, lakes, prairies. It's pristine. Both Kantore and I deal with those types. A lot."

"I didn't know that."

"Yeah. Kantore, he likes Hollywood. I think at least once a year, they're making a movie. That brings good money into Riverton. Over the years, they've really stocked up. Provisioning, what not. They've got the rental equipment, the rental trucks, I heard they've loaded up on the lighting and sound equipment over the years in case the movie production needs backup."

"Smart, I guess."

"For sure. And of course, a police chief sticks around. Not like a mayor, who gets voted in and out every four years. Kantore would have gone through, I don't know, five mayors by now. And what's not to like about his setup? That's good income."

She wondered if Kantore was in on the grift, making his cut off of every rental. The cynic in her guessed yes. "Entrepreneurial of him."

"I hear he even has a guy in L.A. who lobbies for Riverton as a movie location. Just like the Bureau."

"The Bureau?"

"Oh, sure. I've worked with security teams, agents, publicists, PR folks out here all the time. Jackson Hole is very elite. But there's an office in L.A. that manages most Hollywood relationships. I mean, the connection with

Hollywood goes all the way back to Hoover and the clean-cut G-Men brand. Comics, serials, movies. You've heard of his media savvy strategy, right? We need that strong public perception, so they work with us."

She nodded. FBI training included a number of classes on the Bureau's history.

Cross said, "Well, that liaison office is going strong. Gotta protect the image. And gotta have them movies about the Bureau look legit, right?"

"Liaison office?"

"Oh, yeah, it's a whole thing. In L.A. I guess in New York, you wouldn't be too familiar with it. It's got a name. Some acronym." Acronyms were all over the Bureau. He held up a finger. "Something, something P and PA! Stands for something, something Publicity and Public Affairs."

She shook her head. "Learn something new every day."

"So, you were saying about this researcher and the cold case."

Gently, Dom, gently. "Right. Well, in addition to this research, and through publicly available information, she was also able to identify an interesting anomaly in the missing persons data. Of Wyoming."

His eyes narrowed.

"All of these factors together have brought me here."

He said cautiously, "OK?"

He needs to bite. "Roy, I respect the autonomy of field offices. I appreciate that they do a helluva lot better running stuff to ground than the big HQs — New York, DC, whatnot."

He nodded warily.

"And I don't think it's fair that the bigger offices get the recognition more often than not, when most investigations are a collaboration."

He waited.

"So, I believe this particular anomaly should best be looked into, well, from the proper channels in the field office. If they pan out, then you get the authority to pursue it."

"What are you bringing me, Agent?"

"Not to put too fine a point on it, but this state has too many boys going missing. Far outside the normal stats for the rest of the country."

He leaned back in his chair, his brow furrowed. "By how much?"

"Twice as much as the national average."

He rubbed his mouth. "Almost speaks to some kind of… intention."

Like a pedophile ring. That's what he meant. "I am certainly not jumping to any conclusions."

He ruminated. "In my territory."

Right under his nose is what he means. "Roy, I'm only here about my own single case. The data point was useful to me. Now I'm handing it over." Just as she said it, her phone began ringing. It was Mila. She mouthed to Cross, "Sorry," and clicked the line open. "Mila?"

Mila was breathless. "Dom. I'm in Wyoming."

Dom's eyes darted around the small office. "What. Did. You. Just. Say?"

"I'm chasing a lead, Dom. A serious lead."

She waited mutely.

"Jimmy called the NMEC hotline. The year he was taken. I have a recording."

Dom bent her head to concentrate on Mila's words.

"He asked for me. By the nickname he used for me."

She blinked.

"I've tracked down the location of the call. It's in Wind River Basin like we thought. North of Riverton."

"Where are you now?"

"At the location."

Dom looked up and held the phone away from her head, addressing Roy. "How long will it take me to drive to Riverton?"

"Up through Grand Teton, then along Route 26. Probably three hours."

She pressed the phone to her ear. "Mila, I'll meet you this afternoon. Keep me posted on your location." Dom hung up, stood, and said, "The cold case may have just gone warm."

He rose. "I'll call Kantore, let him know you're coming. That your Dodge in the parking lot?"

One hell of an observant field agent. She nodded.

He strode across the office toward the door. "You're not gonna wanna be driving that thing through these mountains. Better you take one of mine. I'll get you a key. I'll get some local guys to retrieve it later. Not a problem. We do a lot of driving out here."

"Oh, I'm not on the clock—"

Turning toward the outer office, he held up his hand and said over his shoulder, "If Barry gives you any shit, you let me know."

Chapter Thirty-Two

The Chevrolet Spark crunched over gravel as it pulled to a stop in the abandoned gas station building on the side of Route 20. A weather-beaten wood sign with faded letters read *Wind River Gas*. Mila switched off the ignition. The ache in her chest expanded painfully and she breathed deeply against the pressure.

She pushed open the door and the roar of Wind River swept through the car. The river hurtled over rocks, forming small crests of white water. On the opposite bank, a train track followed the course of river and disappeared into an arched tunnel burrowed deep into the gray rocks of a steep mountain. In her mind she could hear the sounds from Fi's studio: the high-pitched brakes, the clanging of the steel wheels, the deep, growing rumble of the train as it emerged from the tunnel.

One in a million. Had she found the location?

A car whistled past on Route 20 and she rose from the Spark. She turned slowly toward the building and the long forgotten rotary payphone by its side.

Was that the phone Jimmy used?

She walked slowly to the phone and picked up the smooth handset. It was heavy and cold. For the millionth time, she wondered about Jimmy's temperature. Had he been cold when he had called out to her?

She brought the phone to her ear. There was only silence. The line had long since been turned off. She rested the handset back on the switch hook and hung her head.

This was the location. This was the phone.

Seven years ago, her smart little brother had escaped from the kidnapper's car, raced this phone, dialed the NMEC number he must have seen and memorized from a Missing poster, and called out for her.

Adrenaline raced up her body. She began trembling.

Jimmy, I never got the call! I never got the call!

She slammed her palms against her face, stretched her mouth wide and silently shrieked. The tendons in her neck thrummed.

No! No! No!

Blood pulsed through her arms and her hands quaked against her cheeks.

Jimmy.

Like a wave retreating, the intense burst of physical energy slipped down her body and out her toes. Left behind was only a dazed, empty shell.

She dropped her hands. The sky was blue and endless.

She sank to the ground. Billowy, white clouds wafted high overhead.

Numbness crept up her chest. It felt as if the blue could swallow her up.

She blinked. There would be one less extraneous person in the world.

She took a deep breath. If she disappeared, Dom and

Beecher would be heartbroken. If she disappeared, no one would ever find Jimmy.

She set her hands flat beside her. The gravel was sharp. She pressed them down hard on the small stones until jagged edges almost punctured the skin.

10, 9, 8...

The pain fought through the dullness.

7, 6, 5...

She pushed herself off the ground and rose.

I'm coming, Jimmy.

Mila Pascale did not give up.

Part V

Part V

Chapter Thirty-Three

A whimper emanated from the passenger seat of Roy Cross's Tahoe and Dom glanced over at Mila. It didn't surprise her that the young woman may have been having nightmares. When she'd found her outside the Riverton Police Department over two hours ago, Mila had been talking too quickly. She'd been almost frantic. Dom had sat her down and listened to the impressive series of discoveries. It had been an incredible journey in a short amount of time. Her exhaustion was palpable.

She'd asked, "Have you slept?"

Mila had frowned. It hadn't been important to her.

Dom had reached for her hand. "You're going to need to sleep. And eat."

"OK."

"Let's go in, talk to the sheriff, then find a hotel."

Mila had nodded numbly. The adrenaline had been ebbing.

Together, they had gone into the Riverton Police Station and Dom had held out her Bureau badge to the woman manning the front counter. "I'm here to meet with Chief Shaun Kantore." *Starts with a K, ends with an E.*

The woman had replied smoothly, "Chief's out."

"When do you expect him back?"

"I don't know. He's out at a shoot over in Popo Agie. Sometimes they shoot through the night."

Behind her, Mila had shuffled.

Dom had kept her voice calm. "I'm just looking for some eyes on a missing person case. Maybe someone can have a look at some photos?"

"I'm sorry, Special Agent, but FBI should check in with the chief first."

Mila had turned to the door, her frustration and weakness getting the better of her.

Dom had asked, "How far is this Pope Ag?"

The woman had corrected her. "Popo Agie Wilderness. It's a hundred thousand acres of protected land in the Shoshone National Park. He's up past Big Sandy Trail head today."

"OK? How far is that from here and how long will that take me to get there?"

"Probably about three hours, depending on what kind of vehicle you have."

Another three hours. Roy Cross hadn't been joking when he'd said they did a lot of driving out here.

Mila had slept the whole drive south on Route 789 to Lander and then west on Route 28. She roused thirty minutes before they reached the turnoff for Popo Agie.

Dom asked softly, "You doing OK?"

Mila simply shrugged. Conversation wasn't easy for her.

Dom broached the difficult subject she'd been ruminating on since Riverton. "So, listen. We should talk. There are things I know about missing children cases."

Mila's face was stony. Behind her fatigue, she was resolute.

Dom continued. "We may not find anything. This chase may lead nowhere. That happens a lot. You sense you may be getting close to something, but it slips through your fingers."

Mila stared at the road.

"But sometimes, it's actually worse to get some answers. Because those answers may reveal some very dark things. They may at first be very uncomfortable to deal with."

"Yes."

Dom swallowed. "Not least of which, he may no longer be alive."

"Yes."

"He may have suffered."

"Yes."

"In fact, it is *likely* that he has suffered. That's why people steal children. Mostly."

"Yes."

"I know you've thought about this. We both know what's likely happened to him. He's not that little brother you knew. He's an adult now. An adult with a very bad background over the last few years. He's damaged. No matter how much we want to believe otherwise, he's a different human. I'm just being very truthful with you, Mila. Jimmy is a damaged man now. He may not want to be saved."

Mila had just nodded.

"OK. I know you know all this."

"Yes."

Dom rubbed her eyes before glancing over. "And you

need to know that no matter what we find, I am here for you. One thousand percent. Both Beecher and I are here for you. No matter what we find."

"Yes. Thank you." But her stare never left the road.

"I have a question. I have something you need to think through."

"Yes?"

"How much are you willing to risk to find him?" How far was she willing to go to save Jimmy?

Mila pursed her lips and remained silent for a very long time. Eventually, she said, "Not everything. Not my life."

"OK."

"Not you or Beecher."

Dom nodded. "OK. So the operational rule is that we're not going to risk lives."

"Yes."

"If this goes sideways, you need to remember that. We may lose him. But we're not risking our own lives."

"Correct."

Dom nodded.

A big, brown wooden sign at the entrance to a dirt road had yellow-painted script from the 1980s that read, *Bridger National Forest Campground: Big Sandy*. Dom flashed her badge at the Riverton Police SUV that sat beside the sign and he waved her through.

In the dirt parking lot, she parked at the end of a long line of pickup trucks and SUVs. Nearer the trailhead sat two large container trucks and a long horse trailer that could accommodate at least ten animals. Spilling out from one of the container trucks was electrical rigging, outdoor klieg lights, and three mobile generators. Two horses were tied to the back of the horse trailer. Large, empty packs were on the ground next to them.

There was a cargo truck with a logo *KFS* in big letters with *Film Services* scripted out below. Dom was pretty sure the K stood for *Kantore*. "Looks like being the Chief of Police in Riverton gets you some favors." She turned to Mila. "You let me do the talking."

From the back of one of the trucks, someone had set out a long table of food, utensils, cups, and a large coffee percolator. Nearby, five men in flannels and jeans sat on camping chairs drinking coffee.

Dom waved. "I'm looking for the police chief."

"He's up on location."

"What movie are you all filming?"

A bearded redhead said, "It's a drama. A period piece. 18th century frontier. Settlers, explorers."

"Huh. What's it called?"

"*Two Rivers*."

She nodded. "How do I get up to the location where they're filming?"

He pointed down a trail through the woods. "It's a mile hike that way."

An hour later, the trail gave way to a vista of an open field surrounded by woods and framed in the distance by a mountain range. Green evergreens dotted the foothills. The peaks were frosted white with snow. Big, white clouds were set against an expansive blue sky.

On the crest of the nearest hill, a camera was set up on small train tracks. In the distance, two actors on horses galloped over the ridgeline. Standing around behind the camera were ten additional actors in cowboy or Native American gear.

Dom's phone rang. It was Lea. "Hi."

"Where are you?"

"The film set. I'm surprised I have coverage, actually."

"What film?"

"An old drama. Maybe a Western? What do I know about movies?"

Handlers in real, dirty chaps and stained hats were bringing in horses.

Lea asked, "Any famous actors?"

"I wouldn't know one if they ran over me."

"Mila ok?"

"She will be."

"She with you now?"

"Yes."

"Tell her to take some photos. Tell her to try to get some of the main actors."

Dom scoffed. "You're talking to Dom Walker and Mila Pascale here. You serious?"

"I know, I know, but it may be important later."

"OK."

They hung up.

Dom spotted Chief Kantore. He was wearing jeans under a police jacket. A big cowboy hat was perched on a round head. He waved and started walking through the tall grass toward them.

She said under her breath, "Mila, give us some distance."

Mila sauntered away through the grass.

The chief approached with an outstretched hand. "Special Agent, Chief Kantore. My office said you were headed this way."

She took his hand for a shake, met his strength. "Chief, my name is Domini Walker and over there is Mila Pascale. She's a student at New York University."

"You two from New York?"

"Yes, New York City."

He placed both hands on his low-slung belt. "You're a long way from home."

She looked around with incredulous eyes. "You could say that again. Definitely fish out of water. This is quite a view."

"Oh, yeah."

They paused to take in the scene unfolding of the two riders approaching at a gallop, then veering to the right as they closed in on the camera.

Dom said, "That's pretty cool."

"Yup. These here fellas are straight from Hollywood."

A man behind the camera yelled, "Cut!"

Kantore pointed to one of the men on a horse. "That fella there is one of the stars. And that guy in the seat is clearly the director."

Dom nodded. "We get movie and TV shows filmed across New York. Lots of crews. Lots of those big trailers."

He gazed proudly across the scene. "But nothing like this, I bet. We had the drones up yesterday at sunset. It was a doozy."

"Well, we know traffic jams. I can tell you that."

He took in her measure. "Yeah, I bet. So you came all the way out here to Popo Agie. Looking for me?"

He had zero tells. This guy knew body language. "Well, the station said I had to start with you."

"Yeah, we're funny like that, out here in the boonies. We follow the proper chain of command."

Oh, boy. She waited.

"So, what you got that's so urgent?"

"It's a long shot."

"Well, what you got?"

Dom pulled up her phone and the image of a seventeen-year-old Jimmy. "I'm hoping you may have a lead on this young man. Maybe even know him."

He ignored the phone, looked her up and down. "You came all the way out here to ask me to ID a fella?"

"We know he's been out here. It was worth the ask."

He took the phone and concentrated on the image for a long moment, then shook his head sadly. "I'm afraid you've come a long way for nothing. I've never seen him. I can say that for certain."

"Do you mind if we ask around? I wanted your OK."

He shook his head. "I suppose no harm done. But you appear to be doubting my sincerity. I assure you nobody in Riverton knows that young man. We know everyone here."

She nodded. "Well, we're here, may as well go through the motions."

He shrugged. "Suit yourself."

A shout rang out from the ridgeline. A thin man in a clean Carhartt jacket ran toward Mila waving hands over his head. "Stop that! Stop that!"

Dom moved quickly into a run to meet him before he reached Mila.

Mila stepped backward behind her, slipping her phone in her jacket.

The thin man yelled, "She can't be filming on location!"

Dom held up her hand. "OK, OK. We didn't know that."

He started to protest, but Dom flashed her badge. "FBI. You don't have to worry about leaks. It's fine."

His face contorted.

She held up a hand. "Seriously, I'll have her delete it."

He spun and headed back up the hill.

On their way back to the trail, a young female uniformed Riverton officer closed in on them. "Excuse me!"

Dom and Mila waited for her to catch up.

She wore mirrored sunglasses and her black hair was pulled back in a ponytail. Her boots were weathered. "My name is Monnie Friday. On the Riverton force." She kept her head and hands still, as if to stifle any interest in what they were talking about, and spoke softly as if she didn't want anyone to hear. "Are you Feds?"

"As a matter of fact, I am."

Monnie looked over her shoulder to the ridgeline. Chief Kantore was watching them.

With tight lips, she said, "There's a diner on Main Street in Pinedale. Called Grand Teton. I'll be there in two hours." She turned and walked back up to the ridge.

Chapter Thirty-Four

The sun was setting low over the Hudson River when Owen ordered a delivered meal. The paper bag inside a plastic bag from the delivery guy smelled of Mexican. He set himself up with a plate at the dining room table and started in on the burrito.

His eyes wandered to the laptop, where a photo of a snow-covered valley spanned the screen. It was a property listing for $10 million near Pinedale, Wyoming that had caught his eye. As he chewed, he flipped to the description again.

Private and secluded 3,000 private acres in historic Green River Valley. Expansive views of Wyoming Range Mountains and access to Green River. Ranch complex includes owner's home at 6,000 sq. ft., four cabins, and sizable ranch. Year-round recreational use, including fishing, hunting, horse training facilities, and many winter activities such as cross-country skiing and snowmobiling. Mule deer and antelope migrations. Cattle ranching land available. One hour to Jackson, WY and 20 Minutes from Pinedale, WY.

It would be easy to get away with crimes on such a secluded location.

Owen finished the burrito and wiped his lips. He picked up the burner phone and dialed the number Janelle Wisker had provided for her contact in Riverton.

A male voiced picked up on the third ring. "Horton."

"Mr. Wellington Horton?"

"Yes?"

"My name is John Zokov. I'm calling from New York. Janelle Wisker with Blue Sky gave me your number."

"Yes? What can I do for you?"

"I'm interested in purchasing a fully functioning ranch."

"OK."

"But I want it to be rather secluded. Nothing near a ski resort or a town. Nothing like that."

"OK?"

"And a view of mountains."

"Sure."

"Price range starting at ten million."

"Got it."

"Can you tell me what areas out near you I should be searching?"

Horton said, "Well, you're gonna want to avoid up near Freedom or Star Valley Ranch. And you're not interested in Jackson and the winter crowds there. That doesn't sound like what you're looking for. I've got a couple of areas in mind. There's one outside Pinedale. You want me to send you some listings?"

"Yes, thanks." He rattled off a junk email account. "One more thing, Mr. Horton. I'd like to know some of my neighbors. As you can imagine, that's an important determinant of a location."

"Sure. What type of thing were you thinking?"

Clafoutis had died two years ago. "Can you also send me any similar properties that have been listed and sold in the last two years?"

"Sure. I can get that to you. I'll put that package together and send it through. Give me an hour or so."

Owen retrieved a beer from the fridge and watched the lights across the city. Jamie from Tech had delivered with a long list of properties located the Wind River Basin. Jaimie's script had pulled identifying information for each, including name of owner. Some were individuals. Some were a holding company or trust. His cover note had read, "*Possible mistakes in identifying individuals vs. entities. My script is only so good.*"

Owen's intention was to compare the images from Horton's listings with the images outside Clafoutis's window. If any appeared to match, he would dig into Jaimie's list of owners. Eventually, he wanted a narrowed list of all properties that may have been owned by Clafoutis.

He took another sip. It was going to be a long night.

Chapter Thirty-Five

Pinedale was idyllic. Houses were nestled at the foot of the Wind River Mountain Range. Abundant green trees dotted the landscape. In the distance was another mountain range.

In the Grand Teton Diner on Main Street, Dom and Mila settled into a red booth in the middle and ordered coffees. Thirty minutes later, Officer Monnie Friday parked outside their window and waved. As she entered the diner, she flagged down the waitress, ordered a coffee, and slid into the booth. "Thanks for coming."

Dom nodded. "Sure."

"I'm so glad to see you."

Dom cocked her head. "Oh?"

The waitress set down a full coffee mug in front of Monnie and she glugged down her first sip before she said, "I've got something you should know about."

Dom held up her fingers. "Wait, let's back up. We're here on a cold case."

Monnie nodded. "OK, that's OK. I've got something you want."

Dom held out her palms as if to say, give it to me.

"I think we have a serial kidnapper. Children. Two boys. In the range of eight years old."

Mila froze.

Dom said slowly, "Go ahead."

"One is still missing. The other escaped. The suspect is described as a big man." She explained the case of Anton Norris and Dakota's story, including the details of the house on a dark lake, the items the boy remembered inside. She detailed the coincidence of the film crew at the Mountain View Diner at the same time as the boy.

Mila shuddered.

Monnie glanced to Mila, then back to Dom. "Wait. What is your cold case?"

Dom said, "A missing boy. Seven years now. We think there was a lead in this part of Wyoming, but a long time ago. We also have found some other connects. To this area…"

"What do you mean?"

Dom explained Mila's anomaly.

Monnie exhaled. "Oh my god. Nobody has identified the numbers are off? Not Feds, not local? All these years?"

"Not that we know of, no."

"How do you explain that?"

Dom shrugged. "We don't. Yet."

Monnie's eyes widened. "But it could be a… ring."

"It could be. We're nowhere near that explanation." But the coincidences were adding up in a very uncomfortable way. "You think this big man is part of the film crew?"

"Well, that's what's weird. The first boy went missing three weeks ago. The crew has only been here in Pinedale a week."

Dom and Mila waited.

Monnie said, "He may be part of the local contingent hired on for the shoot."

Dom asked, "How many films get made here every year?"

"Maybe three? Depends. The Wind River Range and high country is pretty iconic and gorgeous. You've got about one hundred miles of peaks. There are something like forty peaks: Gannett, Wind River, Fremont, Wolff's Head, Squaretop, Turret. Lots of big, wide horizons."

"And Riverton is the logical entry point?"

"There's no real entry point. Some come down from Jackson. Others come in via the west side. But Riverton has set itself up as a good launch pad for movie crews. We've got rental trailers, lighting, all that. And provisioning for the food, catering, whatnot. And of course, decent hotels for the working staff. The college also provides good guides and environmental specialists."

"So good for business."

"I mean, yeah."

"And the chief goes up to the locations a lot?"

"He usually assigns one of us to check in. We go on and off. There are only four of us officers."

"Why is the chief up there today?"

"I don't know."

Dom asked, "But you went up today to see if there was a big man?"

"Exactly."

"You see anything?"

"Not today. No. But…" She took a sip of coffee and she glanced through the window. "I heard something. A hunch."

Mila leaned back.

Dom nodded. "We take instincts seriously."

Monnie looked back questioningly.

Dom said, "Why don't you share what you think? It's just three women, having a coffee, shooting the shit."

Mila nodded gently to Monnie.

Monnie took a deep breath. "Lots of the VIPs and stars stay here in Pinedale at big, fancy ranches. They don't stay in the town hotels. There's lots of big luxury out here in Wyoming."

"OK?"

"I heard some of the actors talking about their... I guess you would call it a party."

Dom set her hands on the table.

"This particular crew stays at a very luxurious place called Double R Ranch. It's not the big house Dakota mentioned because the one he saw was dark. No other houses. Isolated. The Double R Ranch is on a lake with lots of neighbors."

"But maybe the big man has been there. To Double R Ranch?"

Monnie nodded. "It's a lead."

Mila coughed.

Dom glanced.

Mila whispered, "What if there are boys there?"

Monnie nodded. "That's what I'm thinking. I don't like the idea of these private parties. They might be bringing stuff -- drugs, boys -- in."

Dom whistled, "That's a big statement."

"I know, I know. But maybe we just ask around. I can take you there."

"I think your chief would be displeased with that."

"Yup."

It was why Monnie wanted Dom there.

Mila's voice was surprisingly strong. "Besides film celebrities, do artists come up here too?"

"Oh, sure. Lots of that."

Dom nodded, as if she'd made a decision. "OK."

Monnie asked, "We'll go?"

"Sure." Dom looked at Mila. "You're going to stay in town. Get some rest." Mila started to protest, but Dom stopped her. "Listen. This isn't the end of the road. This is just one more kink. Stay here. You absolutely need rest. I'll be back when we're finished."

Monnie suggested a small hotel, walkable down Main Street from the diner.

Dom finished her coffee. "Hunches are why we're here. Let's get going."

Chapter Thirty-Six

Mila couldn't sleep. She was supposed to be resting, but her eyes would not close and her mind would not stop spinning. The thought of Jimmy having been so close so long ago jangled her nerves. She didn't have her soothing routines or her steady schedules to calm her. Further, the country surroundings — the expansive landscapes, the soaring mountains, and the sounds of wilderness — were disorganized and unnerving.

She stared at the white hotel ceiling. Dom had been right in the car earlier to caution her. Of course, Jimmy could be dead. Of course, terrible things could have happened to him. Such thoughts often pressed into her mind as scary images and movies of bad, shadowy people hurting him.

Now the bad images took over, rotating as she lay in the strange bed. In one daydream that had been recurring since the day he'd vanished, people burned him with a brand. She could hear his skin sizzle and smell the singe. His scream often startled her. In another, he was dog paddling in a dark lake, trapped under a thick ice sheet. He was pressing his cheek tightly against the ice, his mouth popping opened and closed like a goldfish's, his eyes wide in shock. She was slamming her lacerated fists on the ice and blood was splattering widely.

Tossing on her side, she counted. 10, 9, 8, 7, 6—

She pushed up from of bed, grabbed her jacket and phone, and headed out for a walk. Maybe the ridiculously clean air would clear her head.

The sky was gray and the first kiss of the drizzle banished the terrors. She walked at a moderate pace, one foot placed deliberately in front of the other, along the sidewalk of the main street. If she moved too quickly, it would jack up her heart rate and add to the feelings of anxiety. Better to walk calmly and let the lingering fear dissipate

Forward motion. Keep on moving, Mila.

They were chasing the leads. They were in Wyoming. She had identified the gas station. If someone had stolen him out to Wyoming, surely, it would not be logical for the kidnapper to bring the young boy all this way, only to turn around and head back east.

Because of the rain, she was the only person walking and she started to notice the passing buildings. The lights were on in a hair salon named Big Head. Were they expecting evening customers? A neon sign blinked in the window of a cookie shop, Sweet Treats. Did they list the calories next to their products? The display in the Pinedale Five & Dime was a mix of hobby materials and canned food. Way back when, had everything actually been five or ten cents? Had there once been a soda counter where people had bought ice cream floats? Up ahead was the Feed and Factory Store. Were there canvas bags of corn piled high in a back room?

The door of Feed and Factory opened and two men in cowboy hats emerged. Through the drizzle, the larger, older one had a rolling gait, as if his knees were locked, and the younger, slender one supported a huge, plastic bag on his shoulder.

She smiled to herself. Of course feed came in plastic now.

They headed through the rain at a good clip to a parked pickup truck. The old guy was really big, maybe 6'5", and had to squeeze into the driver's side. The young man moved to the flatbed of the truck and shoved the feed bag deep under a taut cover.

Her even pace had her coming alongside.

The young man sensed someone on the sidewalk and looked up, his face illuminated by the taillights.

Mila froze.

It was Seventeen Jimmy from the Archer's drawing.

The breath expunged from her chest.

Am I imagining this? Was she so tired, she was delusional?

He nodded a quiet *hello* as he stood and moved to the passenger's side.

She couldn't breathe.

Am I going insane?

The passenger-side door opened with a loud creak and Jimmy folded into the seat.

How is this happening?

The reverse lights came on and the pickup inched backward. The license plate was spattered with dry, caked mud. The last three symbols read, *394*.

Have I just found Jimmy?

The reverse lights clicked off and the truck inched forward.

Mila raced to the back of the truck and lunged into the dark space. Her knee slammed the metal bumper. Inside, her fingers grasped the plastic feed bag and she pulled herself into dark space.

The truck rolled forward, gaining speed.

She curled on her side and hugged her knees.

Chapter Thirty-Seven

It turned out, a colleague Lea had known from Quantico knew a woman who worked in the Bureau's Investigative Publicity and Public Affairs Unit in Los Angeles. Lea called her that morning, introduced herself, and explained who she was and that she just wanted some background on the office.

Brigette Jackson was bubbly and enthusiastic. "Sure, Lea, what do you want to know?"

"Can you just give me some background?"

Brigette said, "Off the record."

Lea laughed.

Brigette's voice remained upbeat. "I'm serious."

"Oh. Uh, yeah, sure."

"OK, so the IPPAU helps raise public awareness about the Bureau's work in order to gain the public's assistance in our investigations. Without that support and trust, our jobs would be a lot harder."

"Yeah, I read the website."

She continued as if this were a routine request. "We

work with the television and film industries as well as writers and publishers. We ensure the FBI brand is told correctly. We provide workshops for industry professionals, coordinate interviews, provide fact-checking, consult on FBI protocols and procedures, and on occasion will provide consulting services on TV programs, documentaries, and films."

"What kind of consulting?"

"Pretty much everything you would imagine. How a special agent would approach an investigation, how they would interact with the public and/or a suspect, how they would behave honorably. We make sure the FBI isn't represented poorly."

"How do the industry types find you?"

"We have a number of staff here. And we work with the various agencies. But to be honest, mostly, it's with well-known directors, actors, or producers. We only have so much bandwidth."

"So like famous actors?"

"Sure!" She had the enthusiasm of a Hollywood fan.

"Interesting…" She let the comment hang across the line to intrigue the woman.

"Why?"

"Well, we're working a case…"

"Oh?"

"That is running up against a film being produced in Wyoming. Out of Riverton. Called *Two Rivers*."

"Oh, sure. Lots of great locations in Wyoming."

"Exactly." She waited.

"So…"

"Well, here's the thing, off the record."

It was Brigette's turn to chuckle. "For sure."

"There may be, may be, a connect to a film going on out there. At the moment."

Her voice turned reserved. "OK?"

"Are you able to look up those who may be affiliated to the movie?"

"No. I couldn't do that. Also, we only work with a select few movies."

"But you get requests, surely all the time."

"Only if they're FBI related."

"Ah." Lea gazed out the window. "But you must know a lot of people in the industry. The film industry. I mean, you could ask around, save me some time."

"What are you looking to accomplish? What exactly, Lea, are you asking of me?"

"To know if there's any dirt on anyone affiliated with this particular film. Anything unsavory we should know about. Any lead, even if distant."

"Absolutely not."

"Huh."

"That's gossip. You'd be peddling in gossip."

"I can see how someone in Hollywood would perceive it that way, but in actuality, as a Bureau employee, I'd be doing my investigative homework."

"You'd be looking for salacious rumors."

"I'd be looking for anything that would strike a field agent as good background information."

"No. We don't do that."

"Right, 'cause you're outward-facing. Pro Hollywood."

"We don't do what you're asking because that's not our job. We support the public image of the Bureau. We don't peddle in gossip."

"So you don't support any real investigations."

"That's not fair."

"Take no part in the unfruitful works of darkness, but instead expose them. Ephesians 5:11."

"Did you just Bible quote me?"

"You're fucking right I did."

Brigette hung up.

Lea sat back. "Touched a nerve, did I, Brigette?"

An hour later, an email popped into Lea's inbox. The email was from Brigette Jackson's FBI account. It did not have a subject. Inside, the note was one line: "What's your personal email?"

Lea sent it to her immediately.

Moments later, a new email arrived in her personal inbox. The sender was FI985#1L. There was no subject line or any notes, only a single attachment titled Whispers. It was an Excel list.

The spreadsheet was two columns. The first was a list of a hundred and sixty-seven names. Mostly, if not all, male. The second column appeared to be notes in shorthand.

The first line was a name she recognized. The note next to it read *Nasty in the DMs. Will turn on you.*

Lea had heard about the whisper networks out in L.A. because of the #MeToo movement. Women informally, secretly sharing warnings of men in the entertainment industry who were rumored to be abusive.

Halfway down the spreadsheet, Brigette had highlighted a name. *Bruno Maldives*. Next to his name was a single note. *Creeps on very young men.*

Lea grabbed her mouse and opened up an internet search. She slammed her fingers on the keyboard and wrote: *Bruno Maldives Two Rivers*.

The search came back immediately. It was a press release from Élan Talent Management.

Bruno Maldives signs on to star in Two Rivers.

She opened up the next article — *Bruno Maldives Addiction Confessions* — that had appeared a year ago in *Entertainment News* and skimmed it. According to the star, he'd spent two months in a Malibu rehab and came out clean, fresh, and ready to slay the world. In his words, "Ready to slay the dragons." There was no mention of his name on the Whispers list.

Lea skimmed every article she could find. No mention of Bruno on the list.

She texted Dom. *"Bruno Maldives. Star of Two Rivers. Former addict. Rumor is he's attracted to young men. Very much rumor."*

Chapter Thirty-Eight

Through a light rain, the lights of the Double R Ranch main building — a large, timber structure on a rock wall foundation at the end of a long drive — appeared. It overlooked a pristine lake under a mountain range. Six or seven smaller cabins dotted the property.

Inside, Dom and Monnie found a fire roaring in a huge fireplace and floor-to-ceiling windows. Someone in the rear of the building was singing to a radio. The smell of cooking wafted through a glass door.

Dom leaned her head around the kitchen door. "Hello?"

"Yes?" A round, short woman appeared around the corner. "Hi, can I help you?"

"I'm Agent Domini Walker from the FBI."

Confusion crossed the woman's face.

"I'm here with Officer Friday. We'd like to ask a few questions if we may. Are you the manager here?"

"I cover in the mornings. I'm an assistant. The manager isn't due for another two hours."

"Do you mind if we ask you a few questions?"

"Uh, OK, hold on, let me turn the stove down. Do you want some coffee?"

"That would be lovely."

Dom retreated to the empty main hall and waited.

The round woman returned with a tray of three mugs and had them sit on the deep leather couches. Native American blankets hung over the backs. "My name is Stephanie."

Dom settled the mug in her lap. "Thanks, Stephanie. This is Officer Friday from Riverton Police." She glanced around the room. "This is lovely."

Stephanie smiled proudly. "We try hard."

"You from around here?"

"I've been here ten years. From California originally."

"Well, you're lucky." Dom savored the full-bodied coffee. "We were just over at the film location.

"Oh, right." Stephanie looked relieved. This was all about the filming, not the ranch.

"We understand some of the VIPs stay up here with you."

"Yes."

"Celebrities and whatnot."

She smiled. "Yes."

Dom continued. "We're on a bit of a goose chase. We believe there may be a missing boy around this area. I wonder if we can't show you his photo?"

Stephanie spoke slowly, carefully. "Of course."

Monnie leaned over with the photo of Anton on her phone.

Stephanie took the photo, stared at it intently, then looked up with a blank face and shook her head.

It was a very authentic response. She wasn't lying. "Shame. OK." Dom stood and walked to the window. Dark clouds gathered behind the lighter rain clouds. "The VIPs who stay here. Do they drink?"

"It's a retreat. That does happen."

"And are there drugs?"

Stephanie hesitated. "I suppose."

"Would the guests have, what we would call a 'party'?"

"I suppose yes. Music, drinking, food. Yes."

"And these parties, are they frequented by just your guests or do outsiders also come in?"

Stephanie said slowly, "We do get outside guests who come up."

"From where?"

"I don't know. I don't ask."

Dom turned back to Stephanie. "Have you met them?"

"Who?"

"These strangers?"

"Not really. I tend to go home once the evening sets in."

"But you may have noticed them."

She shrugged.

"Any of these guests young?"

"What do you mean?"

"Any underage guests in the evenings?"

Stephanie clamped her lips shut.

Was that a confirmation? "It could be important."

Stephanie remained mute.

Dom glanced to Monnie with the go-ahead.

Monnie asked, "We may be looking for a larger man. A big man. Does that ring a bell with you?"

Stephanie shook her head.

The front door burst open. A thin woman in a white vest and clean, pressed jeans strode into the living room. "What is going on here?" She glared at Stephanie. "You can leave."

Monnie rose.

Dom held out her hand. "Special Agent Domini Walker and this is Officer Monnie Friday from Riverton Police."

The thin woman grudgingly shook hands. "Ashley Bloom. Élan Talent Management. What is this all about?"

"Do you represent some of the actors on the *Two Rivers* production?"

"That's exactly what I do. We're renting this facility. What is it you want?"

"We just wanted to ask some questions about an ongoing local case."

"Why is FBI here on a local case?"

"There may be some overlap with another investigation."

Ashley Bloom pointed a finger. "Is this about Bruno?"

Well, well, well. Thank you, Lea. "Bruno Maldives?"

"Yes. He's done nothing wrong. He's been clean and sober for a year. I watch him like a hawk. We've been up here two weeks. He's gone to bed every night sober. I can attest to that."

"You are all staying here?"

"Yes."

Dom suggested, "He may have gone out."

"He does not have any keys to any cars."

"How many from the film are staying here?"

"The talent is here. The crew is down the road at the hotel."

Monnie asked, "Are any of the crew staying at other homes? Homes on lakes, that sort of thing?"

"No. As far as I know, the executive producer got a bulk rate and took up the hotel. No reason to send anyone elsewhere." She crossed her arms over her chest.

Dom asked, "How many here?"

"Ten."

"How many at the hotel?"

"Twenty. Ish. I think twenty-three, but I'm not sure."

Monnie asked, "How many locals does the film hire?"

"I don't know. What am I, a producer?"

Dom said, "We're just asking around. Happens to be a case here. Very likely not related to the film."

"Of course it's not related to the film. I mean, you're at the site all day. Surely, you see other folks around? We hire in for craft services, moving stuff around, those horses. Anything technical — the lighting, sound, cameras — is all run by the film's crew."

"Security? Big guys?"

"Not out here. Although now I'm not sure we don't need them." She glared at the two. "Does Chief Kantore know you all are here? Because I'm pretty sure he'd not be thrilled by this interrogation."

Uh-oh. Time to wrap this up.

Monnie soothed her. "No worries, no worries. I think we covered the areas we had to cover. We appreciate your help."

Dom's phone vibrated with an incoming message. She slipped the phone out, glancing at the screen. The message from Mila read, *"I found Jimmy. I'm hidden in the back of their moving truck. License ??? 394."*

Part VI

Part VI

Chapter Thirty-Nine

The pickup truck had driven on smooth road for thirty minutes at a speed that felt between sixty and eighty mph. The raindrops pelting the tarp sounded like rocks slamming against tin. Bouncing painfully against the floor of the flatbed, Mila squeezed the phone to her chest.

At the beginning of the journey, Dom had replied via text instantly. *"Give me truck details."*

Mila had wracked her brain, but she had moved so fast outside the Feed and Factory store that she'd not paid attention. *"Old. Tarp stretched across flatbed. Creaky passenger door."*

"Details of trip."

Her brain was spinning. Thirty minutes at that speed placed the truck a long way from Pinedale. At least thirty miles. *"On paved road. 30 minutes. Probably 60-80 mph. Don't know direction."*

"OK. Save your battery. We're going to try to locate you via your phone. I'm coming to get you."

With each passing minute, she fought panic. This was the worst decision of her life. Except she had found Jimmy.

He was sitting less than a foot away from where she was lying. Maybe it was Jimmy. What if it was a total stranger and she had been badly delusional back in Pinedale? She wasn't prone to delusion, but had she seen him clearly enough to justify impulsively jumping into the back of a random truck?

She contemplated all the possible scenarios once they reached their destination. In the first scenario, the pickup truck would stop and the men would get out and walk away. She would sneak out the back, hide nearby, and take in the situation. She would be alone and defenseless if Dom couldn't find her. She'd have to walk to Pinedale through rural, possible rugged terrain. Unless she was able to retreat alongside the road. At a moderate pace of twenty-minute miles, it would take at least ten hours if her current estimates were correct. At least. Who knew where the truck was going to eventually end its journey?

In scenario two, the pickup truck would stop, the men would get out, and they would come to the back and pull out the feed bag, oblivious to a young, horrendously stupid woman lying deep inside the dark flatbed. After they'd gone, she would sneak out and walk to Pinedale.

In scenario three, they would discover her. What then? Mentally flipping through this the last scenario brought waves of fear and dread. Would Jimmy even know her now? He hadn't recognized her earlier on the sidewalk. Would Big Man Kidnapper grab her? Would he laugh maniacally at having so easily acquired a new victim? Should she keep her identity a secret or come clean? Her brain ricocheted across possible solutions. Should she immediately sprint away? Could she fight them off? Should she try to use her defensive skills that she'd learned at the Red Cross?

If she were an FBI Special Agent, she'd have a gun. If

she died during this ordeal, she'd never be an FBI Special Agent. Had Dom been able to track her via her phone?

The truck slowed and cornered onto a road. Tires hit potholes and sunk into dirt. She bounced hard against the metal floor.

Oh, god, we're on a dirt road.

The truck was going slowly, maybe twenty miles per hour.

She pulled the phone close to her nose. In the pitch black, the dim light cast from the screen almost felt warm against her cheeks. She texted, *"Turned onto dirt road. Maybe 20 mph."*

The truck hit a pothole and she tumbled onto her back, the ridges of the flatbed jamming into her spine. The air was knocked from her lungs. Protectively, she held the phone above her.

The phone vibrated in her hand. Dom had replied, *"We see you. North. Route 352. I'm coming."*

Relief rushed through her, replacing the pain. Dom was tracking her through her phone. She rolled back on her side, swaying with the disjointed movement of the truck, and pressed the phone against her chest. Technology was amazing. Dom was coming to help.

All she needed to do was stay hidden until Dom could find her. Together, they would confront the Big Man Kidnapper and save Jimmy. Together, they would finally end the seven-year hunt for her missing younger brother. Dom and Mila. Together.

The phone vibrated. It was an alert. It had lost reception.

Chapter Forty

Over the speaker phone, Lea's voice was tense. "I've lost her."

Roy Cross's new Tahoe was holding smooth at a steady one hundred and ten miles per hour northbound on Route 352. The wipers swiped silently at high speed and the high-beam headlights bounced off fifty feet of wet asphalt. Tight on her rear, headlights banked off the rearview mirror from Monnie Friday's Riverton Sheriff Ford Taurus.

Dom replied, "Copy. What were the coordinates of the last tower she hit?"

Lea said, "It appears to be about a mile past a turnoff at a road called Pogo Diablo Lane."

Dom plugged in the road's name on her GPS. "Got it."

"I'm staying on the line, Dom."

"No, I need you to call Roy Cross in Jackson Hole and ask him to list the contents of the storage box and the emergency kit in this Tahoe."

"Copy that." Lea was gone.

Dom dialed Monnie. "We may not need it, but what firepower do you have?"

"Only my sidearm. I've called Chief. He's all the way back at Riverton. You want me to call in Pinedale police?"

"Let's find out the situation first. She's made it past a road call Pogo Diablo. What's up here?"

"Not a lot. Mostly unpopulated. Some ranches. A river. Small and large lakes."

Like the dark, unpopulated lake outside the Big Man's house that the young Dakota had seen.

Ten minutes later, Dom's position on the screen map neared Pogo Diablo. She slowed to forty miles per hour as the Tahoe's headlights fought the rain. Monnie stayed close behind. Her eyes scanned for a road. There was nothing.

On the screen, she passed where Pogo Diablo should have been. She slowed to twenty miles per hour. For two miles, there were no obvious roads coming off Route 352.

She pulled over and Monnie pulled alongside. They rolled down windows and Dom asked over the rain, "Did you see any roads?"

"No."

"Let's double back and check again. Slower."

Monnie nodded.

The second pass revealed no roads.

They turned and headed northbound again. Three miles later, two small dirt roads, hidden in the gloom, met at the asphalt, one to the right, one to the left.

Shit. Shit.

Monnie pulled alongside.

Dom grimaced. "I don't know which one."

"We could split up."

"I don't like it."

Dom's phone rang. It was Owen. She jammed open the line.

He rushed to explain. "Dom, I've got something. Near your location are three properties. They are relatively near each other. I think only one road goes in to them."

"Are there any other properties up here?"

He said, "No."

"Facing north on Route 352, are the properties west or east?"

"West. About three miles off the highway. I'm sending a map."

"Copy that. Thanks."

She turned left onto the dirt road.

Chapter Forty-One

The rain pummeled the tarp. Through the back opening of the truck, there was only darkness. Bouncing in the flatbed, Mila held the phone against her chest like a talisman against the devil.

Have I found Jimmy? Maybe. But when the truck stops, prepare to escape.

It had been roughly thirty minutes on the dirt road. That would be well over two hours to hike back to the highway where her phone lost reception. She was not clothed for a hike in this weather. Her jacket was relatively thin and not waterproof. She had no hat. Even her lightweight running shoes would be no match for the dirt road in this weather. Three hours minimum.

Maybe it would all work out. Maybe they would find her in the back, under the tarp, and Jimmy would whoop with joy and hug her. And then Big Man Kidnapper would also give her a hug and explain how it was all a terrible mistake. She would nod in agreement. She would exclaim how thrilling it was to be reunited and that there was no sense rehashing the past. Maybe in some drafty log cabin out here in godforsaken country, they would have a meal together and toast in celebration.

I'm delusional. Maybe it wasn't even Jimmy. Running is the only choice.

The truck slowed around a bend and came to rest. The engine clicked off.

Goosebumps prickled across her skin.

She was in the back of a creepy, creaky old pickup truck owned by a Big Ass Kidnapper, was now off-grid in some wooded wasteland, and Dom was not going to get here in time to save her. She had brought this on herself. That calamitous decision would be either life-changing or life-ending. Terrible. Horrifying. Colossally stupid. Negative ten out of ten.

If they catch me, they will hurt me.

Rain beat the tarp. The truck doors creaked open and slammed shut.

She held her breath, eyes wide on the rear of the flatbed.

Running to escape is the only way out of this.

Five minutes later, she was still alone. They had gone somewhere.

She released a huge breath. With aching muscles, she shimmied to the end of the flatbed and slipped to the soaking ground. Staying low, she inched to the front bumper and peered around. The two men had disappeared into a large, two-story house with a wrap-around porch. Light streamed from two ground-level windows.

Rain slid down the crown of her head and a cold droplet, having made it inside her collar, slithered down her spine.

She scanned the dark surroundings. Through the sheet

of rain and dim moonlight, she could make out a line of thick trees encircling the house and drive. Behind her, the single dirt road was cut through the woods. Toward the rear of the house, there appeared to be a darker open area. Maybe a lake? Maybe the lake Dakota had mentioned?

Wherever this was, it was remote and isolated.

She turned to the rear of the truck, stayed low, and sprinted into the trees.

Chapter Forty-Two

By the interior light of the Tahoe, Dom and Monnie surveyed Owen's map. Five miles ahead along the small, dirt road, three smaller roads split off and led to separate properties, all sitting along the banks of the Green River. Each appeared to have one main building and a number of smaller outposts, perhaps stables or barns. Owen had marked them Ranch 1, 2, and 3 from south to north.

Monnie commented, "Dakota thought it was a dark lake, but maybe it was the river that he saw from the Big Man's house."

Dom warned, "This may be totally unrelated to Dakota."

"You believe that? Two kidnappers of boys from the same area?"

Dom shook her head. "No. But we don't know yet."

Monnie nodded, tight-lipped.

A message arrived from Lea. "*In the box: gun rack with assortment and ammo. Weather gear and first aid with AED.*" Key in *locked glovebox. Glovebox key on keyring."* By "AED," she meant an Automatic External Defibrillators first aid machine.

Dom pointed to the southern property. "Let's try Ranch 1 first."

Monnie said, "Sure."

"You follow me farther along for a bit, then we'll cut our lights and walk the rest of the way in."

Ten minutes later, they parked both vehicles, turned off the headlights, and met near the back of the Tahoe. The world was quiet except for the smacking of raindrops off leaves. Dom pulled open the rear door and crawled to the storage container. From the gun rack, she chose a Glock 21 and a 12-gauge Remington 870 with sling. From the other items, she pulled a shoulder holster and two compact, heavy-duty flashlights. She handed Monnie a flashlight and slipped on the shoulder holster, fastened it, and settled in the Glock. Rummaging through the first aid gear, she handed Monnie the smaller of two kits. She slid from the truck, put on a wool ranch jacket and slung the Remington over her shoulder.

Monnie asked, "You sure we don't want to call for backup?"

"You *are* my backup."

"I mean backup for *us*?"

Rain drenched her head. "No. No time. We need to go assess the situation."

Monnie moved to her trunk and lifted out two stiff cowboy hats. "These will help with the rain."

In the distance, thunder boomed. Dom turned on the

flashlight and aimed the beam down on the dirt road. They took off, with Monnie in line just over her left shoulder. Their pacing matched well and they made good ground.

Monnie said, "I've never fired a gun in a live situation."

"But you've fired on a range?"

Their footfalls were muffled by the wet road. The beam kept their path lit despite the rainfall.

"Yes, sure. But only my service handgun." She lifted her jacket to reveal a Glock 21 in a belt holster.

Dom blinked against the rain spatter. Monnie had been right — the hat helped. "It's enough."

The beam lit up a fallen tree over the road and Dom jumped it in a single bound.

Monnie asked, "What's the plan?"

Good question. The plans diverged. If Mila had remained hidden, it was simply a matter of finding her. If she had been discovered, then it may be a hostile situation. "I don't have one yet. If the pickup isn't here, we fall back, move to Ranch 2. The goal is to retrieve Mila. We inspect all three till we find Mila. We want to get her out undetected, return tomorrow with a warrant."

"What if we don't find Mila?"

"Then we find the pickup truck and I go in."

"No warrant?"

"We have probable cause. Kidnapping. It will hold up." *On second thought.* "I don't care if doesn't."

Monnie asked, "Are you sure?"

Something tickled Dom's brain. There was something wrong in what they were doing. Jogging. Rain hitting the hats. Wet, dirt road. She slid to a stop. "This isn't the right ranch."

Monnie pulled up short next to her. "What?"

"This isn't it. We need to turn around." She pivoted one

hundred and eighty degrees and leaned into a jog in retreat to their vehicles.

Monnie kept close behind. "Wait. Why? What?"

Dom said, "That tree across the road. No pickup went through here recently."

Chapter Forty-Three

Raindrops slapped Mila's face as she sprinted into the nearest trees. Her running shoes and socks were soaked and heavy as they sunk into the soggy ground. She ran ten feet into the woods then slid her back up against a tree, leaned over her knees, and breathed in deeply. Cold was beginning to set in on her arms and legs, but for the first time since Pinedale, she felt safe.

Thunder rolled in the distance. There was only silence from the house.

Now what do I do?

She was alone, near the home of Jimmy and his kidnapper, in a thin jacket and running shoes, in the rain, at night. She pulled out her phone, careful to protect it with her body, and checked reception. There was still no connection to the outside world. She slipped it back in her pocket.

She had no idea if Dom would ever be able to find her. The logical next course of action involved running through the woods, parallel to the dirt drive, back out to whatever paved road or highway they had come in on.

She glanced back to the house. The light from the two windows pooled in warm circles on the wooden porch.

But Jimmy was right here. He was in that house.

She wondered if this was where he'd grown up. Had he been kept this far from town so that no one would know he was a stolen child? Had the Big Man Kidnapper sent him to school under an alias? What horrible things had they done to him?

I can't walk away now.

She wiped rain from her face and gazed at the windows. She could sneak up close and peek inside. She could confirm if the young man was indeed Seventeen Jimmy. Then she could be sure. She blinked against a raindrop.

But what if Big Man Kidnapper catches me?

No, it was better to make a run for the highway and come back later with Dom and maybe Monnie the police officer. Even the next day. As far as Jimmy and Big Man Kidnapper knew, Mila had never been here.

Yes, keep that element of surprise. Come back tomorrow.

She tore her eyes from the house, faced back down the dirt road, and pulled the thin collar tighter around her neck. The soaked shoes squished as she dropped into a jog.

Chapter Forty-Four

Dom held the Glock in her right hand and the flashlight in her left as they jogged silently along the second dirt road in the direction of Ranch 2. They had parked two miles back and were making good time. The slinged rifle slapped lightly against her back and the rain hitting the trees had become lighter. A dog barked in the distance. She wondered what other animals were out here.

Up ahead, the road curved to the right and a thin light appeared from around the bend.

Dom dropped into a walk and Monnie stepped alongside.

She switched off the flashlight. "I think there's a house around that bend. Let's get off the road."

They moved into the treeline. Without the light, the ground was treacherous with dark holes and rocks. Deliberately, they moved slower, picking their footfalls carefully as they followed the road along the bend. Fifty yards ahead, a big house loomed like a shadow against the dark, night sky. Two windows on the first floor were lit, the light pooling on the floor of a wraparound porch. Near the porch stairs was the shadow of a pickup truck.

They came to a stop in the dark shadows of a tree.

Monnie whispered, "It's gotta be them."

Dom said, "I need to check the truck. If it has a tarp and the door creaks, it's confirmed. You stay in the trees. Pull out your service gun. Cover me if they see or hear me and come out of the house."

Monnie whispered, "Got it."

Dom slipped the flashlight into her back jeans pocket. Holding the Glock low at her right thigh, she emerged from the treeline and jogged to the pickup truck. The soggy ground sucked and belched against her boots. Reaching the passenger-side door, she hunched close and with wet fingers, felt slick tarp. Grasping the door handle, she gingerly pulled it up and swung the door outward. It squeaked.

She closed it silently, turned, and sprinted back to the treeline. When she reached Monnie she took in a deep breath. "The door creaked."

Monnie whispered, "That's the big man from the restaurant! That took Anton. What now?"

"I have to get inside. If she's in there, I gotta get her out."

"She may not be in there."

"Doesn't matter. She may be and that's all that matters. You have to cover me."

"OK."

Dom holstered the Glock and stepped out on the dirt road. Yanking the flashlight, she clicked it on. Adrenaline thrummed through her veins. Striding slowly toward the porch, she swept the beam back and forth over the front windows

Forty feet.

She could hear her heartbeat.

Thirty-five feet.

Sweeping the light, she yelled at the windows, "FBI. Approaching the house."

She passed the truck.

"FBI. Approaching the house."

Twenty feet.

The front door opened. The backlit shadow of a large man appeared, his arms and hands close to his body.

She stopped and let the flashlight beam drop to the porch stairs. "FBI. Special Agent Domini Walker. We've received a report of a domestic issue. I need to do a wellness check."

His voice was rough and loud. "Bullshit."

She held out her badge and flashed the beam across it. "FBI, sir. I need to do a wellness check."

"I don't care who you are, you ain't coming in here."

"We need to check on the young man."

"You don't need to do nothin'."

"Sir, let's be calm about this."

He raised his hand and a gun exploded.

Something smacked her shin. *Are you kidding me?*

She dropped the flashlight and dove behind the truck.

She yanked out the Glock with her right hand. With her left, she felt her left shin. Blood was warming her jeans. *Shit.* The burn exploded across up her leg. *Shit, shit.*

Chapter Forty-Five

Mila froze mid-step. *Was that a gunshot?*

Slowly, she lowered her right foot to the ground. The crack had come from behind, near the house.

The thought exploded through her mind. *Was Dom in trouble? No. No. Not Dom and Jimmy. No!*

She spun around and sprinted back through the trees in the direction of the house. Weaving in and out of dark trees, she sprinted along the curve in the road. Her hands slapped rain from her eyes. Sodden shoes slapped the waterlogged ground. Her arms scissored and her lungs burned.

The house loomed in the distance, the light beaming from the two windows and the front door. The shadow of Big Man Kidnapper stood solid in the light from the door. The beam of a flashlight on the ground, the light pointed askew across the drive between the truck and Big Man Kidnapper.

She skidded to a stop by a tree and held out her hand to steady herself. The bark was cold and wet. Her eyes scanned the shadows for Dom.

There. Against the truck, sitting up.

She exhaled. Dom was alive.

From across the dirt road, nearly opposite of her location, there was movement in the darkness. She pressed her left side against the tree and peered through the rain. She couldn't make out a shape.

Just at that moment, the rain stopped.

Squinting, Mila picked up Officer Friday stepping from the treeline and onto the soaked wet road. From this distance, the Big Man wouldn't be able to see her in the darkness. Not with Dom's flashlight beaming across his line of vision.

Officer Friday took a step toward the house.

Mila hissed, "Friday. I'm here."

Officer Friday paused then pivoted. Ten long strides across the drive and she reached Mila. "Are you OK?"

"Yes, yes. Fine. What's happened?"

Officer Friday's voice was tight with fear. "He came out. He shot Dom."

"What are you going to do?"

"I don't know. But I have to do something."

"We need a diversion."

"Yes!"

"We'll both run around the house. Either side. Make noise. We can't let him get to Dom." She pushed Officer Friday off, spun, and sprinted across the road yelling, "FBI! FBI! You're surrounded."

Officer Friday yelled, "FBI! FBI!"

The shadow of Big Man Kidnapper retreated into the house and the door shut.

Officer Friday yelled, "Mila, stay out of sight. Stay behind the trees. I'm going to go get Dom."

Breathing hard, she leaned against a tree. Her legs and chest burned.

Five minutes later, Officer Friday emerged from the treeline near the rear of the pickup and ran low to Dom's position. A minute later, she had Dom up and leaning on her shoulder, hauling her back into the trees.

Mila yelled across the road, "Dom, you OK?"

Dom yelled back, "Yes!"

The lights in the house were doused. Silence descended on the scene.

Dom yelled, "Mila, stay where you are."

But Jimmy was inside.

What if Big Man Kidnapper stole him away again? Maybe out the back of the house? The thought was so unbearable, her chest clenched painfully. She needed to make sure Big Man Kidnapper didn't steal Jimmy out the back.

She pushed off and moved through the trees toward the rear of the house, where darkness opened up over the sound of rippling water.

Chapter Forty-Six

Sitting with her back against a cold, wet tree trunk, Dom asked, "How is it?"

Monnie's flashlight beam was tight on her wound, the medical kit nearby on the ground. "It looks—It looks like a flesh wound. I have to feel it. I'm sorry, it's too dark. I have to feel it."

Dom gritted her teeth. "Go ahead. Do it."

Monnie's fingers pressed into the wound.

The world reeled.

Monnie said, "OK, that's it. It's flesh. The blood is moderate. The bullet is not there. I'm going to stop the bleeding."

A tightness squeezed her shin as Monnie pressed in gauze and leaned her weight into it. Through the pain, Dom asked, "Mila?"

"She's hidden in the woods. Across the road."

"The shooter?"

"He's in the house."

Dom insisted, "You're going to have to get to the Tahoe.

Call backup. Then we need to retreat. I can't walk. I don't think you can hump me out. You need to drive in and get us."

"Agreed. Give me two more minutes to get this bleeding to stop."

Shots rang through the night. They had come from a second-floor window.

Monnie growled. "He's shooting. That crazy jackass is shooting at us."

Dom said, "You've gotta go."

Monnie finished with the bandage and packed up the kit.

Dom reached down with her right hand, slid the Glock from the holster, and laid it across her lap. "When you get to the bend, beam the flashlight back this way. Maybe he'll think we're retreating already."

Monnie crouched above her. "I don't want to leave you alone like this."

"You gotta go."

"You sure?"

Dom barked, "Go!"

Monnie rose and sprinted through the shadows.

Chapter Forty-Seven

Keeping the house to her left, Mila crept through the woods toward the edge of trees overlooking a wide bend of a slow-moving river. With the storm moving past, the moon peeked out from behind a cloud and lit the surface of the water an eerie blue. A small dock extended from below her position. Fifty feet to her left, the dark house and its wide back deck loomed ten feet above the river. From behind her in the woods, an owl hooted.

The back door clanged open.

Mila pulled back into the gloom.

A figure rushed over the deck, raced down the stairs, and ran along the edge of the river toward her.

She crouched down and held her breath.

The light of the moon illuminated his face.

Jimmy?

She rose and stepped from the shadows.

He reached a thin, long dock and leapt the four steps to wood planks. They groaned under his weight. At the end, an outboard motor lay next to an overturned fishing boat.

She yelled, "Jimmy, wait!"

He swerved to a stop halfway down the dock.

She skidded down the wet slope, teetering to stay upright. "Jimmy! Hold on!"

He slowly turned. His face remained in shadow.

She came to stand within twenty feet of stairs. "Jimmy, it's me. It's Lala."

The moon moved overhead, lighting a thin, hard face with almond eyes, straight lips, and a cowlick. *Jimmy!* She couldn't breathe. Memories slammed into her. Jimmy in bed listening to her read him a story, his hand on her arm, his soft breathing, his half-closed eyes. Jimmy pouring jelly from a jar on a piece of toast, the sugary syrup running off all four edges, his eyes twinkling. Jimmy next to her on the couch, eyes wide in alarm as they watched a late-night zombie show.

Say something normal. Don't scare him. Don't be spectrum. She moved to the bottom step and held up both palms. "I'm here. Jimmy, it's OK. It's all going to be OK. I'm here with the FBI. We're going to keep you safe."

Shocked confusion swept his sunken eyes.

She said softly, "You need to trust me. I'm going to make it all OK."

He shook his head. "It will never be OK."

Oh my god, I know that voice. Even though it had aged, she recognized his voice.

Air escaped her lungs. Tears began to fall freely. "Jimmy, it's me. It's going to be OK. Of course it'll be OK."

He shook his head hard. "No."

"It will. I'm here now. I'm never going to let you go again."

His lips were tight. "No."

Her face contorted through the tears, but she kept her

voice soft. "I'm going to take us away from here. We're going to be OK. We'll be together. You and me forever."

His face crumbled. "I can't go."

"Of course you can. I'm going to protect you now that I've found you."

His eyes focused over her shoulder and his voice quieted. "They did things…"

She blinked against streaming tears. Her voice faltered. "I know. I know. It's going to be OK. It's OK—"

Trancelike, he said, "They did things to me. Then later, they made me help them."

Oh, God, say something normal! "Jimmy, listen to me. I've thought about this a long time. I can't imagine what you've been through, but I don't care. I don't care. Do you hear me? There is nothing you could ever have done that will make me not love you."

His eyes were blank. "I didn't want to. But they made me."

Snot was dripping from her nose. She ignored it for fear movement would spook him. "I know. I know, Jimmy. It's OK. I understand. Everything."

"When you find out…"

"I will always love you. I'm your sister. I'm your Lala. We're going to get through it."

His lips tapped together against painful memories. "No one… No one… No one will forgive me."

Slowly, she lifted her hands, palms toward him. "Yes, yes they will. People will understand. It's like you went to war. Bad things happen to people who go to war. People understand that. We bend and move and submit and do things to stay alive. People understand that."

He focused on her face.

Yes! Yes, here I am, Jimmy. She waved her hands in the air to keep his attention. "Sometimes people die in a war. But you stayed alive. You survived. You did what you had to to survive. You. Did. What. You. Had. To. Do."

His face twisted at memories.

Hands still raised, she stepped up on the first stair. "Bad people. That's who did this to you. You didn't deserve this. You are not a bad person. They took your brain and twisted it. And they took advantage of you. That's called duress. Do you hear me?" *Was it sinking in? Was she reaching him?* "Jimmy, I've been looking for you since the day you went away. You and I are going to take a journey to a different life. One where I will look after you. We'll work out all the dark stuff. We'll work it out. You and me."

He blinked, imagining what that future could look like.

The planks creaked under her foot. "You and I are going to find hope. You hear me, Jimmy? We're going to have a future that is bright and hopeful. And we're going to walk away from this place, leave it far behind. We're going to forget it. We don't need to ever think about this place again. Are you hearing me?"

"Yes."

She nodded reassuringly and spread her fingers wide, calming. "Good. Because I've found you and I'm not going to let you go."

In a swift jerk, he shook his head. "It will never be OK." He reached down and lifted the motor. His body sagged under its weight.

What? She leapt toward him. "Jimmy!"

He turned and walked to the end of the dock.

From the front of the house, a second shot cracked through the night.

She was closing in on him. "Jimmy, what are you doing?"

His feet shimmied out over the dock's edge. Dark water swirled below. "I need to move on."

She stopped four feet from him. "What are you doing, Jimmy?"

He wobbled in a turn to face her. In the moonlight, his face was sad but resolute. "I need to move on."

"No." She reached out her hands. "No. You don't need to go anywhere."

He leaned backward.

No! No! Her hands grasped empty air.

As if in slow motion, his body arched out, suspended for a moment in space over the dark water. His almond eyes watched her.

No! No!

He dropped from view and the river swallowed him without a splash.

Chapter Forty-Eight

Leaning her head against the tree, she felt the stiff bark dug into her scalp. It didn't hurt. The searing pain up the lower half of her right leg was too overwhelming. She ground her teeth, reached for the medical kit, and felt around for a pain killer but realized that in the dark she wouldn't be able to identify anything. She dropped her hand.

Overhead, an owl hooted.

At least Mila was safely hidden away in the trees.

She clenched her teeth together.

At least the rain had stopped.

Monnie would drive up a distance from the front porch with the headlights on. She would likely angle the Tahoe with the driver's side away from the house. She would move through the trees to Dom's location and together, they would make it back to the vehicle. Dom would call out to Mila to rendezvous at the Tahoe. Then they would speed back down the dirt road and to safety.

She pressed her scalp deeper into the bark as a distraction from the pain of the gunshot wound.

It was a decent plan, but it wasn't perfect. There were opportunities when they would be visible to the shooter. Also, they were assuming the shooter would stay in the house. If he had used a rear exit to make his way outside, he could be in the woods right now and once Monnie arrived, he could ambush them.

She scanned the darkness.

In the distance, a dog barked.

Then she heard a second noise.

What was that?

She held her breath.

Footfalls on wood.

The big man was crossing the front porch.

She fingered the Glock on her lap.

He must think we've retreated.

She raised the Glock and buttressed her right wrist with her left wrist.

Moonlight peeked through the clouds. She could make out the shadow of the truck. There was only silence. If he was walking across the drive toward her position, she couldn't hear him.

She sighted the Glock on the front passenger's side of the truck.

A dark shadow emerged around the front of the truck.

She pressed her back into the tree and held her breath. There was the shadow of a long gun hung by his right leg. She sighted the Glock on his chest and yelled, "Move back to the house or I will shoot you."

He took a step toward her.

She boomed, "FBI. Get back to the house or I will shoot you."

He took another step.

Her shoulders stiffened. She was a practiced and solid shot.

He raised the long gun.

"FREEZE!"

He set the gun against his shoulder.

She pulled the Glock's trigger.

The crack filled her ears.

The big man fell.

She knew she'd hit the mark. She was a very solid shot.

Chapter Forty-Nine

Mila lunged toward the dock's edge and with one huge stride, was out over the dark, swirling water. Her feet broke the surface and then the frigid wave of roiling black swallowed her whole. With eyes squeezed shut, she doubled over, and headfirst, stroked hard downward in pursuit. Her legs scissored frantically. Outstretched hands were her only guide.

No, you don't, Jimmy! No, you don't!

Her skin burned as icy water swirled past her fingers and pushed against the jacket cuffs. Her hair swirled behind her as she dove deeper, five feet, ten feet.

No, you don't!

Her fingers touched a shoe floating toward the surface. His body must have been angled downward where the motor had landed on his chest as his shoulders hit the river bottom.

With both hands, she clenched the ankle. The frigid water swirled around them. She hand-walked her way up his leg, to his torso and to his chest.

He was still clenching the motor. She yanked against his wrists.

He refused to release the motor.

The air in her lungs began to burn. Clinging to his wrists, she pulled her feet downward through the current and pressed them against his chest. She pushed down on him while she pulled up on his wrist. *Let go, Jimmy!*

The motor shifted. He was losing strength.

Her lungs were scorched. Again, she pressed down against her feet and pulled against his wrists.

He lost tension across his body and his hands suddenly released.

She stroked downward and blindly felt for the motor. *There.* She grasped it with frozen fingers, rolled left, and pulled the motor with her off his chest. She let it fall into the silt.

Her lungs were scalding. Grabbing his jacket, she pulled herself close and worked her way to his head. She wrapped her left arm around his neck, nestling his chin inside her elbow.

There was no more oxygen in her lungs. This was her last shot.

Turning her face upward, with her free hand, she stroked down and finned hard with her feet. They were climbing. Climbing. In her head, she heard the earlier conversation. Dom had said, *"So we're clear. We're going in, but we're not risking our lives."*

She had replied, "Yes. Correct."

"If this goes sideways, you need to remember that. We may lose him. But we're not risking our own lives."

Her lungs were empty.

Dom.

She broke the surface and choked in air. She leaned sideways and yanked Jimmy's head out of the water.

Dom, I got him.

Chapter Fifty

Mila swam hard through the swirling, dark water, hauling Jimmy behind her, toward the bank. Reaching the shallows, she stood in the slushy silt and slowly walked up onto the icy mud of the shore. She grasped under both his arms and leaning backward, heaved his weight from the water. She laid him down face-up and leaned over his chest. He wasn't breathing. *No, you don't, Jimmy.*

She pushed down his soaking collar, jamming two fingers on his carotid artery. There was no beat.

She had an hour. Drowned victims could be resuscitated even if they had been immersed for an hour. An hour.

She yanked at the buttons of his shirt and ripped it open to expose a pale, hairless chest. She placed the heel of her right hand on the center of his chest and interlocked the fingers of her left hand. She leaned over his body and straightened her arms, just as instructed by the Red Cross. Water dripped down from her hair onto his cold, blue face.

Using the weight of her body, she pushed into his chest two inches then let up. His chest recoiled. She pressed again. His chest again recoiled. She gained momentum and began pressing to a steady beat.

Two times every second. 120 times per minute.

From the side of the house, Officer Friday yelled, "Mila?"

She yelled, "I'm here. By the dock!"

"I'm coming."

"Is Dom OK?"

"Yes, she's OK. She's gonna be OK."

"Is there an AED machine in the Tahoe?"

"I think so."

"Get it! Get the AED."

Ten long minutes later, the flashlight beam returned at the top of the slope and Officer Friday yelled, "Mila?"

Her arms were burning, but she maintained the rhythm of the compressions. "Here! Here!"

The shaft of the beam found them and Officer Friday slid down out of the gloom.

Mila yelled, "Do you have the AED machine?!"

"Yes, yes! Here."

"Is Dom OK?"

"She's OK. She's gonna be OK. She took a shot to the leg. It's contained. It's OK. She's in the Tahoe. The big man is dead. Deputies are coming."

Focus. "Do you know how to use the AED?"

"Yes!" Next to her, Officer Friday opened the kit. "Is this your brother?"

"Yes."

Officer Friday pressed the power button of the yellow machine and an automated mechanical voice prompted,

"Plug in the connector next to flashing lights." Officer Friday pressed the plug into the hole, yanked out the two pads, and peeled off the backing from one. "OK. Get clear."

Mila fell back on her haunches and lifted both hands above her shoulders.

Officer Friday pressed the first pad on Jimmy's right deltoid and the second around his left ribcage.

The mechanical voice said, "Shock advised. Charging. Stay clear of patient. Deliver shock now. Press the orange button now."

Officer Friday pressed the orange button.

Jimmy's body jolted.

The machine said, "Shock delivered. Pause."

Mila whispered, "No, you don't, Jimmy."

Jimmy coughed.

Chapter Fifty-One

Monnie stepped through the front door of the big house with her Glock drawn. Two brightly lit chandeliers hung from a high-vaulted ceiling over a large living room with wide views of the river bend. Hunting trophies were scattered across one wood wall. A black bear. A mountain lion. By the fireplace stood a large statue of a cowboy on a rearing horse.

Dakota had remembered a lot of details correctly. Brave kid.

Over her shoulder, she said, "Stay on my left."

A Pinedale sheriff's deputy replied, "I'm here."

Ten minutes earlier, lights had splashed across the trees and the front of the big house as two Pinedale sheriff cruisers had torn up the dirt drive and skidded to a stop.

Monnie had walked toward them with a hand up. "Riverton Sheriff's department. Emergency contained."

A single deputy had emerged from each car and she'd pointed to the big man's body. "I've got one homicide, one shot but stable FBI agent, and two civilians. I need one cruiser to take the injured to Emergency. I need the other officer as backup. We need to go into the house. Possible child kidnapping."

Now, she surveyed the hallways and headed right toward the dark kitchen. Dakota had mentioned hearing the sound of a metal door from the kitchen. She flipped on the lights and scanned the empty room. On the opposite wall, an exterior door led to the back deck. On the wall to her right, an interior wooden door was closed.

She grasped the doorknob and pulled. The door opened easily. Inside was a metal grilled door. She pushed it and it swung open over a dark stairwell.

She pulled out the flashlight from her back pocket and beamed down bare wooden stairs. "I'm going down. Stay on me."

"Copy."

Wooden steps creaked under their feet as they descended. The smell of damp soil filled their noses and a chill swept their faces. She said, "We're looking for a kid." *Anton.*

The flashlight swept the silent chamber left and right. Against one stone wall, ancient wooden shelving units held old trunks lined up in rows. Farther along, two deep freezers hummed quietly.

Their footfalls were silent on the packed dirt floor.

The beam paused on a wood wall cutting the far end of the room with three big barrel-latch locked wooden doors.

Behind her, the deputy whispered, "That's it."

They moved swiftly to the farthest left door and Monnie handed him the flashlight. She reached for the bolt latch, slid it open and shoved the door wide. The beam swept up and into a small, dark room. There was a camp bed and a chest of drawers. The room was empty.

She bolted to her right. "Next one."

She slapped the bolt open and shoved the door wide.

Inside was another empty room.

She bound to the next, slid the lock, and ripped open the door. The beam swept the room. The room was empty.

She exhaled.

The deputy said softly, "Maybe he didn't make it."

Monnie blinked. "He has to be somewhere."

"I mean, maybe he…"

"I heard you. I'm telling you, he's here."

"Maybe he's upstairs, in one of the rooms upstairs?"

Dakota had heard the rattle of the grill door at the top of the basement stairs. "No, he's down here."

She grabbed the flashlight and swept it slowly across the small room. Stepping out into the middle of the chamber, she continued to sweep the light across the shelves and the deep freezers. Deep freezers.

She sprinted across the floor and yanked open the first freezer. The light swept over frozen food. She leapt to the second and yanked open the lid. Again, the light swept over plastic-wrapped food. No little boy.

She turned to the chamber and panned the light over the space. In her ear, her breathing was loud.

The deputy said, "We can come back with dogs. If something is here, they'll find it."

Dom's thought tickled her brain. *We do not quit.*

The beam swept up and down, left and right, over the stone walls; the dirt floor; the cobwebs; the cracked, wooden ceiling beams; and the hanging bare bulbs. "Can you find the lights?"

Two minutes later, five bare bulbs flashed on and dimly lit the space.

She took mental inventory of what she was witnessing. Three locked prison cells with beds. Two big deep freezers full of rations. Shelving units. At least ten old trunks. Dirt floor. Stone walls. Limited lighting.

Where would I hide a boy? Her mind slowed and the beam panned the shelves and the ten trunks. Ten trunks. "Oh, god, no."

She ran to the shelves and pointed to the nearest trunk on the middle shelf. "Help me get this down!"

He moved quickly and together, they lifted the first trunk. It weighed roughly sixty pounds. They set it on the floor and he lifted the lid. A rancid smell escaped. Inside were deep folds of thick plastic.

She held up a hand. "Wait. Only if it's warm. If it's cold, we're too late."

He reached in and felt the plastic. "Cold."

They raced to pull down the next. Again, the strong smell of rotten flesh hit them.

He reached in, felt the plastic. "Cold."

In unison, they both lurched up to haul down the third. It weighed fifty pounds.

She threw open the lid. There was no smell of rot. She pressed her hand to the plastic. It was warm. "Oh, god!"

She scrambled to yank open the folds of plastic.

Inside was a still, emaciated young boy. His long, black hair was slicked to his scalp. His eyes were closed. His lips were cracked with spittle.

She placed a hand on his chest. He was breathing. Unconscious but breathing.

She shoved one arm under his shoulders, the other under his knees, and snatched him from the plastic. She pressed him against her chest. "Go, go!"

Part VII

Part VII

Chapter Fifty-Two

Two Days Later.

Officer Monnie Friday parked the Riverton sheriff's cruiser in the pebble drive of Double R Ranch. The sun was high in the blue sky and a breeze rustled the leaves.

Ashley Bloom of Élan Talent Management stepped from the front door and crossed her arms.

Monnie moved to the bottom of the wide stairs. "Afternoon."

"What's this about? I told you we're wrapping filming today. This isn't a good time."

Monnie took the steps slowly to the top and moved in close to her.

Ashley shuffled backward.

Monnie said, "We've had a crack in a case."

"What's that got to do with us?"

"Don't you want to know about it?"

"Not particularly."

"There's a little boy in the Pinedale hospital. He's been severely beaten and sexually abused. He's in a coma."

Ashley placed a hand across her neck.

"When he wakes up, I'm going to have some questions for him."

Ashley scowled.

"If I find out that your client had anything to do with his current state, I'm going to nail his ass so fast, his head will spin off. Off."

Ashley's mouth dropped open.

Monnie leaned within five inches of her face and said softly, "Once he's in jail, I'm coming for you. For aiding and abetting a known child rapist."

Ashley's face drained of all color. "What? What?" She recovered her composure and a blankness fell across her face. "You'll be speaking to my lawyer is what you'll be doing."

Monnie stepped back and nodded. "Sure. I'll be happy to do that. I'll be asking him to explain the DNA."

Ashley blinked.

Monnie spun on her heel and strode down the stairs. Over her shoulder, she called, "If your client is involved, Ashley Bloom, you better get your affairs in order."

Chapter Fifty-Three

Two Weeks Later

Across the diner's laminate table, Mila slid the menu to Jimmy. "Here you go."

His smiles were still rare, but they were appearing more frequently. Today, he allowed one to creep across his face and reach his blue eyes. "You've made your guess?"

She smiled in return and nodded. It was their new tradition. She would review the menu and guess the items he would order.

He asked, "Sweet?"

She played coy and winked. "I won't tell."

"Salty?"

She shook her head, "I'm not telling. You have to decide."

A week earlier, she had explained that in all her dreams about finding him, she'd wondered if he would prefer sweet foods, like lemon meringue pie, or if he would prefer salty plates, like eggs and toast.

His face had fallen immediately. Seventeen Jimmy was sad a lot.

She had pushed on. "It was mostly good dreams. I knew I would have to find out."

He shook his head. "But you have no idea what I like."

"Now I don't. Not right now, I don't. You're right. That's sad. But life is long. And I will learn. And that's what we'll do. We'll learn." *There were so many things she would learn about his life. So many. But life was long and she didn't need to know now.*

A small moment of hope had crossed his eyes. He'd ventured to ask, "What foods did you dream I liked?"

"Pies and ice cream."

He had nodded.

"And maybe salty. Like French fries."

He'd opened his mouth to speak.

She'd interrupted him with a raised finger. "Don't tell me. Let's guess each time we go for a meal."

He had nodded seriously. "That's a good idea."

Before she could censor herself, she'd whispered, "It's a ten out of ten good idea."

His face had softened and his eyes lit up. He'd repeated with a whisper, "Ten out of ten."

He remembered her oddities! A warmth had swept through her. Around Jimmy, she did not have to *pretend* to be normal. She could speak naturally. Authentic Mila was accepted.

In the diner, he picked up the menu and perused the items before looking up and starting to softly laugh.

Laughing! She hadn't seen him laugh since they'd returned to New York. "What! What?"

His laugh was growing. "Waffles with syrup, and fried chicken and French fries."

It was sweet and salty all at once. Locking eyes with him, her chuckle soon turned to loud laughter.

Relief and joy swept through them. Tears stream down both their faces as their laughing rang out in the diner.

Later, they stood on Bowery Street outside of Zills Production. She looked over at him. "Are you sure?"

He nodded. "It'll be good for me to connect with people. Sympathetic people."

"Did Eileen say that?" Since their return to the city, he'd been going every day to Owen's therapist, Eileen Bremmer, as they sorted out his recovery plan. Owen had also gotten Jimmy a criminal defense lawyer to guide him through his assistance to the Bureau and the local Pinedale sheriff's department.

He nodded.

She motioned toward the hot-pink door. "Fi helped find you. She is definitely sympathetic."

"OK."

"How do you feel?"

He blinked and stared at the door. "I don't know what I feel."

Eileen had said his emotional actualization and agency would take a long time. It was going to be a long healing journey. "That's OK. We'll just try out this introduction. If it goes south or you panic or if you feel bad in any way, we leave. That's the thing: You have control. *You* are in control."

He repeated the phrase hesitantly. "I'm in control."

She squeezed his hand. "You are in control."

He nodded gravely to her. With more confidence, he said, "I am in control."

Together, they pushed through the hot-pink door.

Chapter Fifty-Four

Five Weeks Later.

Monnie Friday sat at her desk, chewing a piece of sugar-free gum and scrolling through her preferred news sites. There had been another mass casualty shooting in Alabama and she paused to read the details. As law enforcement, she shook her head in disgust. Thoughts and prayers were useless.

At the bottom of her screen, a new headline scrolled past on the ticker. *"Bruno Maldives arrested."*

She clicked the link.

Bruno Maldives, the star of the last year's breakout hit, Roommates, *was arrested by LAPD at his home in Beverly Hills this morning. He has been charged with statutory rape, sodomy, and molestation of a minor. No further details are available at this time. A representative from Élan Talent Management, Ms. Ashley Bloom, is quoted as saying, "We have no reason to believe these allegations are true. We have known Bruno for over ten years and have nothing but respect for his work ethic and raw talent. That said, if these allega-*

tions prove to be true in a court of law, Élan will be dropping Maldives as a client. We give no quarter, no safe haven, to these types of crimes."

She had been interviewed several times by LAPD about Maldives. There was an ongoing investigation out in Los Angeles but they were also keen to hear about her suspicions of the connections between the Big Man with the stolen boys in the basement, the parties at the Double R Ranch, and Bruno Maldives. Relief washed through her.

Next to her forearm, her cellphone vibrated. It was a message from FBI Special Agent Domini Walker. *"Looks like they have enough to charge him. I hope they nail him to the wall."*

She thought of Anton's limp and bruised body as she had carried him from the basement and from this morning's hospital visit as he'd lain in the big bed next to the beeping life support machine. She exhaled and typed a reply, *"Me too."*

"You done good, Officer Friday. You make Riverton proud."

She texted, *"We don't quit."*

Dom replied, *"We sure don't."*

Next in the FBI Agent Domini Walker Series

vinci-books.com/thequietshroudofsnow

A child vanishes into the storm.

Can Dom Walker bring her home before the trail goes cold?

When a murdered girl in Central Park leads to a missing child, FBI Agent Dom Walker uncovers a trail stretching from New York to Alaska—an abduction tangled in cover-ups, corruption, and power that kills to stay hidden.

Turn the page for a free preview…

The Quiet Shroud of Snow: Prologue

Many years ago

Wrapped in a thin beach towel over a damp swimsuit, Dom Walker tapped her bare feet on the cold aluminum bench at the Thomas Jefferson swimming pool. The blue and red striped ribbon, heavy with a round gold medal, scratched the skin at the nape of her neck. Her stare was fixed on the group of eight-year-old boys on the far side of the aqua-blue, Olympic-size pool. A meet official in a black track suit leaned over the boys, assigning lanes.

Beecher, her eight-year-old brother, was part of the huddle, but he had stepped backward, as if to distance himself from the group and his right heel bounced against the cement. Lifting his right hand, he began scratching his left forearm--hard.

Dom stiffened. Something was wrong.

Beside her on the bench, her father, Stewart Walker, was watching the mixed fifteen-year-old relay happening in the pool, oblivious to Beecher's distress.

Beecher's knee bounced rapidly.

Dom leaned forward. Skinny, blonde-headed Beecher was a foot smaller than the other seven boys in the huddle. *Why was he so tiny?* She willed Beecher to look her way.

Beecher turned and caught her gaze. His lips were trembling, trying not to cry.

She held the stare of his wide, scared eyes.

His brows scrunched low, and he gave a tight shake of his head, as if saying, *I can't do this.*

She nodded and rose. *I'm coming.*

Stewart Walker noticed her movement and followed her gaze.

She took a step toward the bleacher stairs.

Her father touched her arm as he stood. "I got it. You stay here."

She sat back down as her father pressed past and moved down the steps.

By the huddle, the official clapped his hands and pointed to the starting blocks. Walking in a loose line toward the end of the pool, the gangly boys stretched their arms over their chests and swung them in wide circles. Beecher, trudging stiffly at the back of the line, broke into rapid blinking.

Dom squeezed the damp beach towel tightly around her chest.

Stewart Walker rounded the pool and waved to the official. Moving to meet Beecher, he put his arm around his son's shoulders and leaned in to speak softly. The two whispered for a moment before her father straightened and patted Beecher between his shoulders.

Beecher nodded, wiped his face, and looked to Dom.

She raised her eyebrows. *You ok?*

He nodded back. He was better.

When her father returned, he said, "He'll be ok."

She stammered, "The other boys. They are not his age group. They're huge."

"At the last minute the official graduated him up to the nine to ten age group."

She said, "He only turned nine last week. That's not right."

Stewart Walker nodded.

In the pool, the relay race had finished, and the swimmers clung to the wall, catching their breath.

She looked to her father. "What did he say?"

Stewart Walker said, "That he wanted out of the race."

Beecher's group filed toward the swim blocks.

A chill tingled Dom's skin. "What did you say?"

"I told him he could walk away. No one was forcing him to swim. He could walk away before the race or just quit working hard during the race."

Beecher took position behind the lane eight starting block.

The official blew a long whistle, and the boys stepped onto the blocks. Four of them circled their arms like seasoned swimmers. Beecher rolled his shoulders.

Dom pulled the towel tighter.

The official yelled out, "Take your mark."

Stewart Walker continued, "I told him that he was only racing against himself."

The line of boys bent at the waists, stretched straight arms toward toes and grasped fingers around the front edge of the blocks. They locked their stares at the far end of their lanes. Beecher's gaze was grave but not fearful.

The official held up the electronic horn.

The boys froze.

Dom held her breath.

The blare bellowed across the complex.

The boys exploded off the blocks, their legs powering them low through the air. Beecher's arms were extended rod straight with his biceps tight to his ears.

All eight bodies plunged through the water's surface.

Dom exhaled.

Next to her, Stewart Walker said softly, "I told him he might come in last. He might come in third. But if he quit, he'd never, ever know. Wasn't that worse than trying?"

The Quiet Shroud of Snow:
Chapter Two

The call had come in twenty minutes before 11 P.M. Through the heavy falling snow, it had taken FBI Special Agent Dom Walker thirty-two minutes to reach West 77th Street on the Upper West Side across the street from the Museum of Natural History. Glancing at the large edifice through the windshield of the Lancia Fulvia Coupé and the fog of snow, it felt like a lifetime had passed since the Hettie Van Buren case. So many cases. Too many cases. Reaching to the tiny back seat, Dom lifted the official dark-blue Bureau parka. The forecast said the snow would continue through the night.

Outside, the city's noise was muffled along the side street and the air was clean, as if the two inches of accumulated snow had sponged up the city's smells. From the car's trunk she grabbed a pair of gloves and a hat. She also shoved a large flashlight into her coat pocket. Unlocking the gun case, she slipped the Glock into the belt holster at the small of her back.

Crossing West Drive, she pushed an earphone into her

ear and pressed *1, the programmed speed dial for Lea Peck, her Staff Operations Specialist. At twenty-four-years old, Lea was lightyears beyond her chronological age. She was an accomplished athlete who also had an extraordinarily intuitive mind for research.

Lea answered quickly. "I'm headed into the office. Where are you?"

Dom said, "Just walking into the park."

"I heard they have a body."

"That's what I hear too."

"Why call us in for just a body?"

NYPD handled homicides day in and day out. The Bureau only got involved in murder cases that had national security, organized crime, or high-profile aspects. Dom said, "Not sure. The request came in from NYPD on the scene."

Lea said, "Huh. Odd. You talk to Fontaine yet?"

Yves Fontaine was the Assistant Director in Charge, or ADIC, of the Bureau's New York office. In an unusual and temporary arrangement, ADIC Fontaine was acting as Dom's direct supervisor. He was a good manager: he gave Dom and Lea a lot of independence. Mostly because they got things done. That was what they did. They got missing kids back alive. Dom replied, "Not yet. I'll let him get some sleep."

She cornered right at the entrance to the park and strode down the sloping, freshly snow-covered sidewalk. Golden light from old-fashioned streetlamps glinted off the large, airy snowflakes that grazed her lashes.

Lea asked, "Did *you* get any sleep?"

Only four hours earlier, Dom had been dismissed by the New Jersey field office from a child kidnapping case in Princeton. She'd been there as extra eyes to a waning investigation. She replied, "Some."

Lea insisted, "Tell me."

"Probably two hours."

"That's what I thought. That's two hours sleep over the last twenty-four. I'm tracking you now."

When it came to lack of sleep, there were limits to what a body could endure. During an investigation Lea tracked Dom's sleep. At seventeen hours without sleep, Dom's reflexes began to be impaired. At twenty-four, her cognitive abilities were impacted. At thirty-six hours, her mind played tricks and her ability to articulate or see was reduced. Their agreed limit was a combination of a few sleeping hours in a thirty-hour period. Dom replied, "OK."

They fell into a comfortable silence.

Dom's footsteps crunched on West Drive heading south toward the Oak Bridge. Dispatch had said the scene was in the Ramble, a wooded walk through the center of the park. Ahead, a pointer with its nose to the snow raced across a pristine white field, his owner following behind.

In her ear, Lea asked, "This snow came out of nowhere. You wearing boots?"

Dom said, "I had them in the trunk. Got them out earlier."

"Good. Might be a long night."

A light breeze sent the top layer of snow swirling, and the moment felt cinematic, almost romantic. She wondered what FBI Special Agent Owen Whyte was doing this time of night then quickly reprimanded herself for the distraction. *You're on the job. Stop thinking about Owen.*

As if reading her mind, Lea asked, "Have you seen Owen this week?"

A flutter tapped Dom's chest. Strong, funny, sexy, smart Owen Whyte, who brushed the hair from her eyes, held her hand as they walked down the street, and looked into her soul. In the storm, she allowed a small smile, and a warmth spread through her chest. She liked him. A lot. "Not this week."

Lea responded, "Hmm. Maybe you should see him."

Why is everyone suddenly so interested in Owen? Just the day before, her brother, Beecher, who read her like a novel and knew that it had been years since she'd been interested in anyone, had broached the subject.

Standing in their kitchen, Beecher had said, "Owen's been around a lot lately."

She'd given him a single raised eyebrow.

"You like him a lot." Beecher grinned and wagged his eyebrows. "Potentially, you're even falling in...you know what."

Her stomach clenched in yearning and fear. She shook her head and clamped her lips.

Beecher smiled. "You know, that's not a bad thing."

She scowled.

"Maybe you could even think about opening up to him a bit."

"We—"

He held up a hand. "I know. I know you gotta go slow because of the case."

The New York FBI office was building a case against the current LAPD Head of Internal Affairs for his involvement in the murder of Stewart Walker, their father. To ensure justice was meted properly, Fontaine had insisted Dom stay far from the investigation. By a stroke of good and bad luck, Owen had been assigned to the case as the forensic accountant. Hiding their developing relationship and avoiding the subject created a complicated needle to thread.

Beecher continued, "I get it. I know you two aren't

talking about the case. But what about opening up to him about personal stuff?"

She protested. "I *am* opening up."

Beecher placed his hands on his hips. "Oh, yeah? Have you told him about Mom?"

Shortly after their father had been killed, their mother abandoned them. It was a source of pain and deep shame. She replied reluctantly, "Some."

"Does he know Mom couldn't engage? That she sat mutely? That she didn't wash us, feed us, hug us?"

She glowered at Beecher. It wasn't as if Owen was hanging out his own dirty laundry.

Beecher squinted at her, waiting for an answer.

She relented. "Not the details, no."

"That the kids in high school said Dad was a dirty cop, that they didn't want your 'crook kooties,' that they parted like waves in the hallways as you passed, that you sat alone at a lunch table for four years, that you didn't have any friends because you couldn't bring them home to our empty apartment?"

She held up her palms. "All right, all right."

He crossed his arms over his chest. "That we had sleeping bags on bare mattresses? That we didn't have heat in the winter? That we took warm showers at the Y? That we got our clothes at the thrift store? That we saved for months for that new pair of Nikes my freshman year so the kids wouldn't torture me like they had you? Does he know any of that stuff?" Beecher's voice quieted. "Does he know that you raised me?"

She looked away.

He pondered her for a moment. "Our history is not something to be ashamed of. We survived. That's strength." Walking over to her. "You realize communication is the only way to make a relationship thrive, right? You can give it up to someone else. I promise you'll still be Dom Walker, big, bad FBI agent." He hugged her before turning, opening the fridge, and leaning in. "What's the worst that could happen? You guys fall in love and then he dumps your ass?"

Her stomach had knotted.

Over his shoulder, he had said, "As just noted, you've survived worse."

Across the lake, the skyrise buildings on 59th Street looked like ghostly silhouettes behind a gauzy curtain.

In her ear, Lea repeated, "Maybe you should see him this week."

Dom retorted, "It's fine."

"Have we defined what *it* is yet?"

Because Dom and Owen had decided to go slow, they saw each other only once a week. Went to dinner or a movie. Other than heated make-out sessions, they'd held off sleeping together. "Do people actually define that type of stuff still?"

Lea chuckled. "Listen, tough chick. You're not a teenager who refuses to be defined. You grew up calling it 'seeing someone,' 'dating someone,' 'sleeping with someone,' or 'involved.' So, what *is* going on with that man?"

It was getting harder to protect herself from her feelings for Owen. If he changed his mind, the pain would be manageable. She wasn't deep enough for a break up to be agonizing. But the point of no return was closing in. And it was terrifying. "I'll get back to you on that."

Lea's voice was smooth as butter. "He is working you just right. Slowly, slowly catch the tiger."

Dom snapped, "Shut it."

Big, round flowerpots stood sentry on the bridge's thick cement walls.

Lea said, "I've just made it to Javits." She meant the New York FBI Headquarters Javits Building north of the Financial Sector. "Hit me up with you've got something."

"For sure." The line closed.

On the other side of the bridge, a path led into the Ramble's woods and Dom picked up the trail of footprints heading deeper into the dark woods. Streetlamps threw bright circles every twenty feet. Tree branches, heavy with snow, bent low. Ten yards farther, the footsteps moved off the path, over a foot-high fence, and into the dense woods. Up the slope, a bright light beamed between tree trunks. She clicked on the flashlight and stepped over the fence.

Twenty yards up the hill, a uniformed patrol officer held the beam of a flashlight for a male NYPD's Crime Scene Unit detective who was clicking together a large tripod crime scene lamp. A second Crime Scene Unit detective, a woman, was snapping together the tensile posts for a ten-by-ten white tent. By the looks of their progress, they had been on the site ten or twenty minutes.

The three glanced down the hill as Dom's beam announced her approach. She spoke in a clear voice. "Special Agent Dom Walker."

The three nodded. They knew what *Special Agent* meant.

Dom stepped next to the uniformed officer as the lamp clicked on, illuminating a forty-foot circle around a small mound covered in an inch of snow. It was the size and shape of a body that had fallen backwards up against the slope, toes pointing skyward, the soles facing downhill.

The officer clicked off his beam and introduced himself as Sylvester D'Amico. He was short and stocky with a round face, soft skin, and puffy eyelids and he wore a thick, blue winter coat, an NYPD blue knitted cap, and big gloves. "We got the call an hour ago. A walker had his dog off leash.

Said the dog wouldn't return so the guy followed him up here, saw this, called 911, didn't wait around." D'Amico pointed to the male detective by the light. "NYPD Crime Scene Unit Detective Hall."

Hall was tall, broad shouldered and had a bright red beard. He nodded.

D'Amico indicated the woman wrestling the tent over the body. "That's Detective Kettle. Like a teapot."

Kettle was short and curvy, and a braided tail of long blonde hair hung down her back, catching snowflakes. Her blue eyes squinted through the light and she and Dom exchanged a glance of recognition. Women in the field stuck together.

D'Amico continued, "My partner and I have been here forty minutes. He's scouting the area. Kettle and Hall have been here about ten."

Dom clicked off her flashlight and waited silently beside D'Amico as the tent was set in place over the body. This was an NYPD homicide. No need to play the heavy Fed. But she still wasn't sure why she was here.

D'Amico asked, "Don't you guys usually arrive in a pair?"

The use of 'you guys' was a soft swipe at the Bureau. It could have been harsher. Territory was almost always an issue between local law enforcement and the Bureau, but Dom was more understanding than most Agents. If an NYPD officer trampled on one of her investigations, she'd be irked too. "It's common but not required. I mostly work alone in the field."

In fact, she had a long history of alienating colleagues. Her remote demeanor and relentless drive turned off most. She liked to think of both characteristics as her superpowers, rather than deficiencies, but they made her a difficult partner. Each of her managers had eventually released the leash, allowing her to hunt like a fox hound on cocaine. It was only recently that she'd acknowledged the benefits of the odd team of Lea, Mila and Owen. Maybe Beecher was right: FBI Agent Dom Walker didn't have to always be such a lone wolf hard ass.

With the tent and light situated, Kettle reached into a tool kit, pulled out a large round brush and stepped to the mound. Gently, she dusted snow off the face.

D'Amico and Dom leaned in.

The victim was a woman. A young woman.

Kettle said, "Teen by the looks of it." She brushed the chest clear of snow. "Gunshots, looks like two, spaced apart, both to the chest. My guess the shooter was close." She peered under the body, "It happened after the snow started. There's an inch underneath. Recent. Rough guess, two hours ago."

From the top of the hill, a beam bouncing left and right came toward them through the dark trees.

Looking up, D'Amico said, "That's my partner." He lifted a radio from his belt and clicked the line open. "Anyone?"

A male voice replied, "No."

D'Amico shook his head, clicked on his flashlight, raised the beam and steadied it on a spot twenty feet away under a large pine tree. "That's why you're here."

Dom blinked.

D'Amico said, "There are footprints. In the snow. Small ones. A kid. Moving away from the scene. My partner went to see if he could find anything."

Adrenaline slammed through Dom's veins. Two hours ago a child had run alone into Central Park to get away from a murderer.

The Quiet Shroud of Snow: Chapter Three

Dom clicked on her flashlight, strode swiftly around the tented crime scene, and jogged up the hill through the falling snow to where D'Amico's beam was holding steady.

A uniformed officer emerged from the line of trees and headed for D'Amico's spotlit point.

When they reached the light, she said, "Dom Walker, FBI. Talk to me."

"Officer Tracy," he said through heavy breathing, winded from his trek through the woods.

Tracy's beam replaced D'Amico's and Dom leaned in. Footprints headed away from the crime scene. The prints were small, not an adult's, and were already filled with an inch of fresh snow. Her heart raced.

Tracy swept his beam eastward into the woods. "I lost the tracks maybe 100 yards out there. Near a huge boulder. I looked around but couldn't find anything."

She turned to race after the child's tracks, but Tracy stopped her. "Wait." Through the swirls of snow, his beam landed on a spot near his own feet. "Here."

She stepped over the child's prints toward him. A second set of footprints covered by an inch of snow ran parallel, heading in the same direction. The prints were large. An adult. Her chest constricted. The perp had chased the child. She looked up at Tracy.

Tracy confirmed the worst, "The prints connect about thirty yards out. I lost both tracks at the boulder."

There was no time to delay. Another inch of snow in the next thirty minutes and the tracks would be completely covered. The evidence would be lost. She yelled down the hill, "Detective Kettle, can I get you up here?"

Kettle was quick to close the distance and Dom pointed to the footprints. "We've got two tracks. A child and an adult. We need them protected from the snow. I'll need both sets documented with size references."

Kettle waved her hand for Dom to go. "I'll take care of it. Go!"

Dom spun east, locked her beam on the small child's prints, and took off at a run.

Snowflakes were dropping heavily now, gaining weight as the storm intensified. They slapped her face and eyelashes. Jogging, her beam bounced from the child's tracks, across trees, and through openings between trunks. Forty yards into the woods, the tracks merged. The perp had followed the child's footprints like some grotesquely reversed Hansel and Gretel. *Please don't let me find a body.*

She ducked under branches heavy with snow and zig zagged through the trunks and underbrush. Her boots felt heavy and her breathing was hard. *Please let this be a kidnapping.*

Her beam swept across a large round mound. It was the boulder Officer Tracy had mentioned. Slowing, she stepped up to test the slipperiness of the rock, but the wet and sticky surface held her boot steady. She scrambled to the top of the boulder where it hung above East Drive. Looking over the open space of Cedar Hill, she swung the beam to the huge snow-covered conifers in the distance. Slowly, she spun a full circle, letting the beam splash over, up and down, looking for tracks. Nothing. There was only the quiet muffled sound of snow. *If this is a kidnapping, I can rescue a kid.*

If this were a kidnapping, the clock was on. The early hours of a chase were the most critical to the recovery of evidence: torn clothes, dropped mittens, scrapped skin or blood. Over 90% of recovered children were found in the first 24 hours of abduction.

She raced down the side of the boulder and circled the light across the ground. Nothing. She sprinted around to the left. Nothing. She spun and circled back to the right. Nothing. Had both the child and the perp jumped off the top of the boulder? Steadying herself against the icy rock, she leaned out over the cliff and shone the beam at the base of a 30-foot drop. The visibility through the falling snow was terrible and she couldn't see anything.

Screw it. She tossed the flashlight from the cliff. Falling through the darkness, the beam circled across flakes then hit a snowbank and sunk, a light saber beaming below the surface. She squatted, dropped on her backside, and slid feet first from the cliff. The ground raced upward. Her boots dropped through a low snowbank and slammed into frozen ground. Pain shot through her shins as she rolled into her right shoulder. Her bare hands pressed into the snow. Her knees jammed against the ground, and she grunted.

The pain in her knees and forearms eased as she pushed herself up. The flashlight beam beckoned. She raced to fish it out and slash it left and right. *There.* Twenty feet to the north the snow's smooth surface had been disturbed. She raced to the indentations. *Yes*. These were landing spots of both the victim and the perp. Her beam shone up the incline. *There. Skid marks.* The child had raced to the left around the boulder. The perp had followed. Both had slid down the slope. The landing cavity in the snow left by the child was small in diameter, maybe two feet around. The cavity of the perp was twice as large.

Her beam picked up the tracks where the two had run north. She leaned into a run. *Please don't let me find a body.*

Her breathing was hard. Her thighs were burning with the effort of lifting the boots through snowdrifts. Snow pelted her eyelashes.

The prints weaved between a grove of trees. Ten yards later, she reached an open area with a chain link fence around a parking lot and a work shed. By the end of the fence there was long trench in the snow.

She slid to a walk and stood over the trench. The perp's outsized prints were two inches from her booted toe. *What is this?*

Her heavy breathing pounded in her ears as she stared at the long trench and two sideways big prints. *What is this?*

Her mind slowed as the realization formed. The running child had hit a patch of ice, slipped, skidded, and landed on the ground. The big man had approached and stood over the child.

A chill ran up her spine as she swung the beam in a large circle. A single track of big prints reached a long dirt path protected from the snow by thick pine trees overhead. The big man's tracks ended. *No!*

She leaned on her knees, closed her eyes, and imagined a young child looking up into the devil's face. A grip tightened around her chest. The big man had picked up the child and carried them into the falling snow. The child was now lost in the vastness of New York City.

Snowflakes dropped around her, muffling the night noises.

She opened her eyes to the darkness, took one last deep breath and straightened. At least she hadn't found a body. She imagined her father whispering, *"That's right. My Dom doesn't give up that easy."*

Pulling out her phone, she turned on the video recorder and hefted the flashlight to her shoulder to act as a spotlight. She would film the entire route back to the crime scene for evidence. Because it had only been two hours since the child had been taken and FBI Special Agent Dom Walker was going to get them back.

The Quiet Shroud of Snow: Chapter Four

Twenty feet above the crime scene, under the large pine tree, Detective Kettle had covered a section of the tracks of the child and the big man with a thirty-foot sheet of plastic. Dom leaned over and lifted one end. The tracks were clear. The plastic had protected them. She let the corner of plastic drift back to the snow.

She gazed upward, letting the falling snow land on her face as she caught her breath. She was tired, her knees ached and her fingers were still frozen despite having pulled on gloves. None of that mattered. A child, terrified and alone, was out there with the big man.

She pulled out her phone and dialed ADIC Fontaine's cell phone. He picked up. No matter what time of day or night, he always picked up. His gravelly voice was soothing. "Talk to me. What have you got?"

She said, "Sorry to wake you."

"What have you got?"

"One deceased. Teen girl. Looks like a second, young

kid ran from the scene. Footprints in the snow into the woods. A man followed the kid. A big man."

"Abduction?"

"Yes. I'm working on the assumption the kid is alive."

Down by the tent, Kettle saw her and began to walk up the hill.

Dom asked, "You sure you want me on this?"

"Yes, get it started." Then he was gone.

Kettle reached her and nodded back into the woods. "Find anything?"

Dom nodded. "There was a chase. About two miles. Then the perp picked up the kid and walked away. I lost the tracks."

"You get photos of all that?"

"I took video of the tracks along the entire route." Dom pointed to the plastic sheet. "Thanks for this. The snow will fill in everything else soon."

Kettle said, "I've got good photos."

"Can you do me a favor?"

"Name it."

"Can you take some measurements of the span *between* the prints for both the child and the perp? I'm going to try to figure out when they were running and when they were walking."

Kettle nodded. "I'll send it all via Brixt." It was the latest cloud database software used by investigators. Among its many capabilities, it ensured an unbreakable chain of custody.

They walked together through the snowfall back down the hill.

Under the tent, more areas around the victim had been cleared. A black, puffy coat was open to expose the wounds to the chest. A red scarf was wrapped around her neck. Black snow boots extended from the legs.

D'Amico asked, "I take it you didn't find the kid?"

She shook her head. "The perp grabbed the kid. Headed away from the scene."

D'Amico said, "A kidnapping. A Bureau issue. We'll take the homicide."

She nodded. "I've already gotten approval." Her phone pinged with a text from Lea that read, *"I'm ready for you."* She stepped away from the lighted area.

Lea answered, "Hey."

"We've got a child who ran from a murder scene. Now presumed kidnapped." Dom sniffed against the cold. "Fontaine's given approval to chase the kid. The deceased is a teen female."

"Got it. We be small but mighty." It was an inside joke between them. Together they had a success rate far beyond many of the more heavily resourced teams in Javits.

Small but mighty. Dom glanced up the hill. "Two sets of footprints lead eastward through the Ramble's woods. One small. One large. Very large. The kid saw the murder, so now our perp's gotta get rid of the witness. Looks like the perp caught up with the kid just as the Ramble ends up north. Near a fenced-in shed. Looks like the kid slipped and fell—"

"The big man monster picked the kid up?"

"Yes. That's the working hypothesis. I lost the tracks there."

"Hold on. I'm looking at a map. Yes, yes, some kind of work area. That's your shed."

Dom said, "At that point the big man is carrying the child. He'll need to get to a street."

Lea asked, "Wouldn't the kid be screaming?"

"It was late, in a snowstorm. Hard to see and sound is muffled."

"But still, what if big man makes it to the street, wouldn't someone see him with the kid?"

There was a long pause before Dom said, "He probably knocked the child out."

"Fucker." For all Lea's Baptist background, her curses were rarely mild. "He can't go north because it's the 79th Transverse." She was examining the map for an escape route. "He could go east, west, or south."

Dom said, "What's the most direct route out of the park?"

"Here, yes, there's a path from the shed along the north side of Cedar Hill out onto Fifth Avenue below the Met. The simplest answer is likely the best."

"Agreed."

"So now he's on the street on Fifth Avenue. Let me see. There's the 77th Street Subway station on that corner and southbound buses."

Dom hypothesized, "Maybe he grabs a taxi. He can excuse the prone child as if it were sleeping."

Lea replied, "Plausible."

"There may be NYPD surveillance camera—"

"At the intersection. Hold on, let me look that up."

As Dom waited, her eyes scanned the area. It was a secluded location, up amidst the shrubs and trees, far from the yellow glow of the path's streetlamps. Why had the teen and the child been here in the first place? In the middle of a snowstorm? Her mind slowed. That question wouldn't help them find the perp. She blinked. Was there a better question? *How* had they gotten here? That answer would better help them find clues. She said softly, almost to herself, "Can we trace how they got here?"

Lea heard her. "Yes! Yes! If we can't chase the perp, let's back track on the victims. There are surveillance cameras all over the park."

Dom said, "Yes. What route did the victims use to get to this location and can we get to those security cameras?"

Lea's voice took on an excited pitch. "The Central Boathouse complex is south. Directly south of the Ramble. There's a restaurant there with a patio. They'll have security. If the victims came up from the south, they would have passed there."

Dom fished out her wallet, stepped back into the tent's light, and handed her card to D'Amico. "I'll be in touch. Call me anytime. I don't sleep."

He nodded.

With the phone firmly against her ear, she strode down the hill toward the Ramble's snow-covered path. Stepping over the low fence, she glanced north. The clock was on. "We're taking a chance they didn't come from the north."

Lea confirmed the statement. "Yes."

Dom turned south. "It's a chance we'll have to take."

"Yes. I'll wake someone up to get us into the Boathouse."

Dom broke into a jog. "I'm on my way."

Grab your copy...
vinci-books.com/thequietshroudofsnow

About the Author

H.N. Wake spent two decades across Africa, Asia, and Europe, working first with the U.S. State Department and then with a global bank. Her expertise in human rights, democracy, and sustainability gave her a front-row seat to some of the world's most significant complexities.

In the early 2000s, Wake returned to the States to further her career. It was during those early mornings before the sun rose that she first attempted to write and, over time, discovered a powerful release for her demons.

Her books are marked by snappy dialogue, relatable characters, and razor-sharp research. Critics rave that her savvy, fast-paced thrillers resonate with a healthy dose of zeitgeist and feel as if they have been ripped straight from the headlines.

When she's not crafting edge-of-your-seat narratives, H.N. Wake is off traveling, sailing, or scuba diving—with many of her adventures sneaking into her plots. She currently calls the East Coast home, sharing life with her husband and their Tasmanian devil dog.

You can find her on a select few social media platforms.

www.ingramcontent.com/pod-product-compliance
Ingram Content Group UK Ltd.
Pitfield, Milton Keynes, MK11 3LW, UK
UKHW041837111125
464979UK00004B/115